Out of Order

Out of Order

BETTY HICKS

SCHOLASTIC INC.

New York Toronto London Auckland Sydney
Mexico City New Delhi Hong Kong Buenos Aires

ISBN 0-439-89036-5

12 11 10 9 8 7 6 5 4 3 2 1   6 7 8 9 10 11/0

Printed in the U.S.A.   40

First Scholastic printing, September 2006
Book design by Jennifer Browne

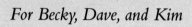

For Becky, Dave, and Kim

Lily

"Your name is a flower for dead people."
What kind of mean person would say that?
Somebody in my family. That's who.

Mom – Frank
     Eric
     V
     Lily
     Parker

I'm the one second from the bottom.

Before Mom married Frank, I was on top, the oldest. Then, right after the church organist hit the last note of "Here Comes the Bride," I dropped.

Eric, my new stepbrother, is at the top but doesn't want to be. He reads too much, says strange things like, "Lily, you mixed a metaphor," and writes secret stuff in a worn-out brown leather book. Normal teenage boys do not keep diaries. Do they?

V, my stepsister, is brilliant, popular, and seriously

beautiful. She's the one who says my name is a flower for dead people.

"No, it's not," I tell her.

"Yes, it is." V looks me straight in the eye. Even when she's being flat-out ugly, you notice her movie-star face. That, and her chocolate hair, cut super short—like a boy's.

"Morticians put them on the tops of caskets." She hisses all her s's at me. Exactly like a snake.

I've never been to a funeral, so I wouldn't know. "Put what on the tops of caskets?"

"Lilies," she says, slithering into her favorite pose—the one with her shoulders thrown back and her chin so far up in the air it looks like somebody snagged it with a fishhook.

"So?" I ask, even though I *have* always wanted a more rock-solid name—something with more grit, like Roxie or Jo. "What's so bad about that? Don't undertakers—"

"Morticians," she corrects me.

The last time I checked, morticians and undertakers were the same thing. Aren't they? Now that I'm not the oldest anymore, I don't feel as sure about everything.

"Okay," I say. "Morticians. Don't they use roses and lots of other flowers, too?"

"Yeah," she says, "but mostly it's lilies."

Her sneaky grin tells me that something mean is on its way, and I know I should shut up, but I can't.

"Because they're pretty?" I ask.

"No. Because they're massively odorific."

"Odorific?" I repeat, wondering if that's really a word. But V is the smart one, so she should know.

"It's the only flower that reeks enough to cover the stink," says V.

"The stink?"

Even I know how stupid I sound—nothing but an echo. And, even though I suddenly get what's probably coming next, I can't stop myself. "What stink?"

Her green eyes light up. "The dead-person stink, dummy. Like I said, *Lilll-eeeeee*," she drawls my name practically into the next county, "your name is a flower for dead people."

I want to hit her.

Instead, I speed-scan my brain for the perfect words to stab her back—a hopeless plan. The search engine in my head is way too pitiful, and the best I can come up with is, "V stands for vomit!" which I shout, even though I know good and well that V stands for Vanessa.

She stares at me. A look of disappointment or pity— who knows which? Then she laughs. "That is so third grade."

I'm in sixth grade, so clearly, this is not a compliment.

Five minutes pass before, finally, I have a killer comeback, but she's long gone.

I wish I'd said, "Well, you should know all about funerals."

ERIC

Journal Entry #167

My writing sucks.

"The scared kid ran and ran, until his lungs lost the battle, all the air squeezed out of them like an accordion."

I wrote that for an English assignment. Mr. Jackman said it sucked. Actually, he said it was a mixed metaphor, which is teacher code for sucks. He said it jumbled up music (the accordion) with war (the battle), and you can't do that.

Why not?

Leo Tolstoy wrote books with hundreds of pages. I bet he mixed a metaphor somewhere.

War and Peace *alone had 1,136 pages.* That *is one heavy-duty topic.*

What could I write?

Acne and Zits? *They aren't even opposites.*

What is the opposite of zit?

Journal Entry #168

Tolstoy wrote this famous first line:

"Happy families are all alike; every unhappy family is unhappy in its own way."

Three years ago, I wouldn't have had a clue what that meant, but I know now, because I'm living it.

BEFORE:

The Stone family—Me, Mom, Dad, Ben, and V, living in Chicago—we were happy enough, just like any other regular family. Lame jokes. Lake vacations. Dumb homemade Mother's Day cards.

AFTER:

Ben died, and all that stuff moved out of reach.

We were pitiful. Not like homeless families with no food. Not like those movie-star families, either—the ones who give Porsches and piles of money to their kids and everybody ends up on drugs.

No. Our pain wasn't hunger. Or the lost feeling you get when the grown-ups in charge are stupid.

At first, it was disbelief. While leukemia was busy trying to kill Ben, we just never thought it would.

Ben could beat anything.

He was that super-fast antelope you see on the Discovery Channel— the one who always gets away from the lion.

But he didn't.

We felt numb, empty. If I were a writer, I could describe it better. Four people living together. Each of us alone.

So—Mom split. For L.A.—Land of Amnesia.

Dad moved to North Carolina. Land of the Evans family—Mary Beth, Lily, and Parker.

Midwest meets South

They're my new stepfamily now—part one of a group package that includes a bunch of aunts, cousins, and an old man named Papa Bud who is a greeter at the Spicewood Cafeteria. He's OK, but embarrasses V so bad she gets hives.

Adjusting to a new family is tough, says Dad. Help your sister. Be a leader.

Who's going to help me?

So—now my family is bigger, but bummed in a whole new way.

Thus, the Tolstoy:

"Every unhappy family is unhappy in its own way."

I've named it off-track-trauma.

Like we all got derailed riding an iron monster across the frozen Siberian permafrost. One second warm inside the passenger car. Next second tossed in a snow bank, no clue which way is up.

Get a load of that, Mr. Jackman! A perfect metaphor from the superlative pen prowess of Eric.

"Off-track" is about trains.

"Derailed" is about trains

"Iron monster" is a train.

Yes! I can write.

The second I got home from babysitting at the DeVaughans',
I went straight to Dad's workshop—the one he built to keep all
his tools and projects in. Helping him while he makes things has
been my favorite thing to do forever.

The backyards in our neighborhood are lush grass carpets of
weedless fescue—carefully cut by lawn services. Some even
have Japanese water gardens with funky statues, but our house
has a workshop and a vegetable garden in back. Nothing tacky—
the outside of Dad's workshop is wood, but it's painted to
match the slate-colored stucco on our house. And Dad and I
keep the garden weeded so well you can see perfectly straight
strips of dark, clear dirt between the rows of okra, squash, and
tomatoes.

"Dad!" I called out, throwing open the workshop door. The
whirr of his electric sander buzzed the air around my ears with a
familiar vibration. The raw smell of sawdust tickled my nose.

"Hi, Princess!" His face lit up. Dad has a little-kid look about
him. Thick, messy brown hair that makes him cute, and round
wire-rimmed glasses that make him look smart.

"What're you building?" I shouted over the buzz.

You wouldn't think a guy who owns a chain of successful

fresh-food franchises would be a master craftsman, but he is. He can build anything.

Then I saw Lily. Lounging in the Adirondack chair that Dad made for me to flop into while he hammers and saws. When I'm not handing him nails or helping him sand, I love to chill out and just talk to him.

"A new dining table for the kitchen," he answered, switching off his sander and shoving his dark hair back with his wrist, leaving a sawdust smear across his forehead. "Eric claims ours is too crowded."

"That is a fact," I agreed, waiting for Lily to clear out of my chair.

"Homework?" Dad asked.

I shot Lily a *that's-my-chair* look. "Some algebra."

"Guess what?" Dad beamed as if he'd just won a new ten-inch, sliding, compound miter saw. "Lily wants to grow something in the garden."

"Yep," chirped Lily. "Sunflowers."

"In our garden?" I was stunned.

"Right," said Dad. "How about you show her how to plant them?"

Lily gazed up, expectant. From my chair. She had on a sloppy T-shirt, so big it practically swallowed her whole.

"But Dad, it's a vegetable garden."

His face tilted down, examining the sanded tabletop as he stroked his fingertips across it. Slowly he raised his eyes and said, "As far as I know, Princess, there are no laws prohibiting the growth of flowers in a vegetable garden."

Only this time when he said "Princess," it was not remotely the way he'd said it sixty seconds ago. That "Princess" had been *Hi, I'm happy to see you!* This "Princess" was *Man, I'm ashamed to even know you.*

Okay. Damage control. In my most helpful voice, I cooed, "Sure, Lily. That'll be cool. But sunflowers are so big." I pictured them towering over my Boston lettuce. Or blocking the sun for my tomato project. "How about pansies?" She seemed like the pansy type, but to my credit, I didn't say it.

"Thanks!" Lily exclaimed enthusiastically—from my chair. Then she added, "I'd still like to try sunflowers, though."

Lily Evans—little Miss Sure-of-Herself. Where had she come from all of a sudden? It reminded me of how bossy she'd been back when Eric and I first moved into her territory almost a year ago—when she was the oldest and had the answer to everything.

Dad smiled encouragingly at her, as though she'd just said she'd like to become president.

"Whatever," I muttered, closing the door quietly on my way out.

I thought about checking my tomatoes. I've planted fifty tomatoes in tiny plastic pots. When they're big enough, I'm going to sell them in the neighborhood and buy soccer balls with the money I make.

The family I babysit for, the DeVaughans, have a son who's stationed in Iraq because of the war. He says the kids there love soccer, but need balls. They call them footballs.

I didn't want to look at my plants now, though. One—I was too annoyed at Lily. And two—noisy, nasty bugs called cicadas were buzzing everywhere. I hated stepping on the dead ones. They crunch. So every day I rake them off the gravel path, and every day new ones show up.

I trudged up the back steps, hoping to find Eric so I could tell him the good news about a new table for the kitchen.

Which Eric would I find?

Three years ago, he was Mr. Goof-off. Always joking. Then Ben died—of leukemia—and it was like Eric disappeared into a cave. We all did.

We moved from Chicago all the way to Charlotte for distance therapy. Except Mom. She moved all the way to L.A.

She needed glitz. Dad needed topsoil.

It's been three whole years now, and I miss our brother, Ben, as much as anybody, but I got back to normal. Why can't Eric?

He's totally turned into Mr. Quiet Guy. No friends. Always reading. Not 'zines or *Sports Illustrated*. No. He reads Tolstoy and Dostoevsky—two dead Russian guys who wrote books longer than anyone with a life will ever have time to read. What I wonder is—when did they find time to write fifty million pages?

And why does Eric like them? It's as if he got an overnight flash: Be old. And boring.

I swung the back door open. Would Mary Beth, the invisible stepmother, be in the kitchen? It seemed to me she was always either cooking or gone.

I can cook.

I've told her that. Eric and Dad love the spaghetti sauce I used to make with turkey instead of ground beef. But apparently, she thinks I'm Parker's age—nine. And useless.

I'd like to fix her hair. She wears it in two styles: in-a-hurry uncombed, and in-a-hurry twisted up and clamped in the back.

I glanced around. No Mary Beth. Instead, Bubbles—Parker and Lily's cat—stretched sleek and powerful in her usual spot on the kitchen window seat. She nailed me with a steely-eyed stare. How did she ever get tagged with a name like Bubbles? I wondered. Gray with black stripes, she looks like a small tiger that's been dyed the wrong color.

I reached for a can of Fancy Feast tuna and pulled up the tab that opens the lid. A hiss of air cabled fishy smells across the room to Bubbles, who raised her royal head and sniffed. As I spooned kitty chow into her blue ceramic bowl, I heard hoots of laughter bursting from the den.

Eric Stone. My brother. Laughing.

It sounded so great I got goose bumps.

"Eric!" I flew through the kitchen and into the den so fast I almost booted Snowman into a chair leg. Eric's little white mutt is round and chubby, but he had spread himself so flat on the floor, he could've passed for roadkill.

Eric sprawled on the floor beside Parker, whom he's renamed Mud Boy.

Now, *that's* a name that fits.

Parker is a total mess—leaf pieces and a portion of a stick stuck in his matted hair, scabs everywhere, and bare feet that, I swear, have never been washed.

Eric and Parker were punching each other and giggling like a couple of five-year-olds. A dozen Star Wars action figures covered the floor, and *SpongeBob SquarePants* blared too loud on our new, flat-screen TV.

My fifteen-year-old Tolstoy-reading brother was watching a kiddy show with my nine-year-old stepbrother . . . and laughing.

"What're you guys watching?" I asked expectantly.

"Oh. Hi, V." Eric threw a quick glance in my direction. "You wouldn't like it."

A weird, pink, amoeba-looking blob was accusing SpongeBob of giving all the other ocean bottom–dwellers a bad name. Some slinky spineless creature belched a bunch of bubbles and SpongeBob cursed, "Oh, tartar sauce!"

Parker laughed and shoved Eric on the arm. Eric laughed so hard he actually snorted.

"That's funny?" I asked.

"Yeah," they chuckled in unison.

"No way!" I declared with total confidence, throwing my shoulders back and lifting my chin.

Eric waved his hand idly, dismissing me like a gnat.

★

When I came out of my room an hour later, my algebra was finished, but my feelings still hurt. Lily was prancing down the hall toward me, beaming like the sunflower she couldn't wait to plant.

I told her that her name was a flower for dead people.

Parker

"My name," Parker said to his mom, "is Mud Boy."

"Fine," said Mom, pushing her hair back from her face. "Pick up all your action figures and take them to your room —*Mud Boy*."

"Aw, Mom."

"Aw, Mud Boy."

"You're no fun."

"You, on the other hand, are a *blast*," said Mom, kissing him on the top of the head. "Now, get your stuff out of the den."

"It's not hurting anything," said Parker.

"Wanna bet?" Parker's stepfather sauntered into the room wearing a Wake Forest sweatshirt sprinkled in sawdust. Parker thought he looked exactly like Harry Potter— but older. He even wore round glasses.

"Yesterday I sat down to watch the news and got stabbed in the butt by a two-inch light saber," said his stepfather, absentmindedly brushing dust off his sleeve.

"You said *butt*!" shouted Parker. "You're going to get it! Isn't he, Mom?"

"Frank, honey. Please try to use grown-up vocabulary in front of the children."

"Oh, right. Sorry. Parker—"

"Mud Boy," Parker corrected.

"Mud Boy," said his stepfather, "your needle-nosed light saber almost punctured the sensitive flesh on my derriere yesterday."

"What's a derriere?" asked Parker.

"A butt," Frank answered.

"I give up," groaned Mom.

"Does that mean I don't have to pick up my toys?" asked Parker.

Mom rolled her eyes, which was her way of saying, *Duh—of course you do.*

"Eric has to help," Parker argued. "He played with them, too."

"I doubt that," said Mom and Frank both at the same time.

Eric slouched by on his way down the hall.

"Tell them!" shouted Parker.

"Tell them what?" mumbled Eric from beyond the doorway.

"That you played with my stuff."

Eric sauntered back into the room. He leaned his tall, thin body against the door frame, closed the fat paperback he'd been reading, and examined the clutter on the floor.

Tugging nervously on the bottom of his black T-shirt, he stretched it over his long, baggy gym shorts.

"Yeah. Okay," he said matter-of-factly.

Frank and Mom traded looks. Mom's showed surprise. Frank's hid something else. Irritation?

"What?" Parker blurted, eyeing them both angrily. "You thought I was a liar?"

Frank turned to Parker with concern all over his dust-streaked face. Even his glasses were sprinkled with tiny particles. "No, Parker. Of course n—"

"Mud Boy," sighed Parker, wondering how clearly Frank could actually see him through the grit.

"Of course we don't think you're a liar," Frank continued. "We're just surprised that—"

"That I was playing Star Wars?" said Eric, tossing his book on a chair and bending over to scoop up a tiny Luke Skywalker and three hooded jawas.

"Well . . . yeah," said Frank, removing his glasses and cleaning them with a wad of his sweatshirt.

"Come on, Mud Boy," muttered Eric. "Let's get this mess out of here."

"See!" Parker exclaimed with satisfaction. "*Eric* knows my name."

Parker thought Eric was about as cool as it gets. Only, for some reason, he was a lot more fun when nobody else was around. In fact, this whole new stepfamily thing wasn't bad, except for some of the new rules. Like not recording over a TV show without having to ask a million people if it's theirs. Or taking turns talking at the dinner table.

Not that the whole idea hadn't freaked him out the first time he'd heard about it. Mom had sat him down, all serious like, facing him on the sofa and holding his hand.

"I didn't do it," Parker had announced.

"Do what?" Mom asked.

"Whatever it is you look so worried about."

"Parker, honey," she'd said. "You like Frank, don't you?"

"Yeah, he's pretty fun."

"Well, good. Because Frank thinks you're pretty fun, too."

"He said that?" Somehow *pretty fun* didn't sound like something Frank would say.

"Honey," said Mom. "Frank and I want to get married."

Maybe that hadn't been the very next thing Mom had said, but it was the part he remembered. That and the funny feeling in his stomach. Followed by all the questions that flooded his brain. Where will I live? Will Eric and V live there, too? Will they boss me like Lily does? Will this make Frank my dad? What about my real dad? Will Mom still read me books at bedtime? And go to movies on Saturdays? Or will she be with him all the time? Does Lily know yet? I bet she hates it. She won't be the oldest anymore. But I'll still be the youngest. I'll always be the youngest.

"Sweetie," said Mom. "What are you thinking?"

"I think it's a bad idea."

Mom's face sagged so far Parker thought it might slip right off her head and slide across the floor.

"We'll have fun," she pleaded, almost in a whisper. "You've always wanted a brother. Remember? And a dad who doesn't live a thousand miles away, and—"

"A *younger* brother," said Parker. "I wanted a younger brother."

"But Eric is great. And he'll have his license next year. He can take you—"

"You don't get it, Mom." Parker looked her in the eye. "I've always been the youngest." He crossed his arms and squeezed them against his ribs as if he were suddenly cold. "Now," he grumbled, "I'm going to be even younger."

The muscles in her mouth twitched. "Oh, Parker," she said gently, wrapping her arms around him.

He was pretty sure she was trying not to laugh, and it made his face flush red-hot as he buried it in the softness of her sweater.

"Everything's going to be fine," Mom soothed. "You'll see."

And she was right. Everything was fine.

V didn't boss him much at all. She bossed Lily instead.

Frank let him hammer stuff with all his leftover wood scraps. Mom still read to him, not quite as much as before, but enough. He had a cat *and* a dog. And Eric was even better than a snow day.

ERIC

Journal Entry #169

"I'm growing older but not up."—*Jimmy Buffet*

He got that right.

Journal Entry #170

Dad's on my case.

Again.

"You're the oldest. Act like it."

Maybe he didn't say that, but he thought it. I heard it in his voice.

If only I could talk to him. About Ben. About how I'm not Ben.

Is this new family supposed to replace him, or is that still my job? For sure, I could use the extra help. But there's too many people. I have to stake out the TV hours ahead. Dinner's so jammed I can't cut a pork chop without somebody catching an elbow—or an attitude. Six of us. We need a bigger table.

Eight if you count Bubbles and Snowman. That cat and my dog get along better than the people. Which is not to say they get along well. Just better.

And what's the deal with V? All of a sudden, my sister's seriously whacked. Bosses everybody. OK—Let <u>her</u> be the oldest.

Lily—she's OK. Just quiet.

Mud Boy—he's the best. One very cool little kid.

If Ben were here, could I go back to being me? Or would it just be more flipping crowded?

Lily

I will not call my brother Mud Boy.

Call me Saint V.

I bought Lily sunflower seeds—with my own money—and I showed her how to plant them.

I even squeezed my tomato plant project closer together to give her a spot with the best sun.

"I'm very proud of you," Dad told me.

My insides bubbled up—happy. Even better than when I get to buy new clothes.

And Dad doesn't know the real reason I'm growing tomatoes. That's going to be a surprise. He's bound to think that sending soccer balls to kids in Iraq is an awesome idea.

Ben was one of the best soccer goalies in Chicago—before he got sick.

And my plants are already so green and leafy, I'll make a fortune—enough for lots of balls. I plan to charge two dollars a plant, which is a lot, but that's going to include me actually planting them in the yards of the people who buy them. Besides, it's a good cause.

And—who knew—Lily's not so bad. A little stubborn maybe, but smarter than you'd guess if you just went by the grades she gets in school.

She actually saved Snowman's life.

He'd been flying around the backyard in a total frenzy while we planted Lily's sunflowers. He was leaping up, over and over, like he used to do before he got too old to catch a Frisbee.

Only now, old or not, he was trying to snatch buzzing cicadas right out of midair.

At first I thought they were locusts and we'd been stricken with a miniature biblical plague, but Dad said no, they were cicadas. I figured they were just one more weird North Carolina phenomenon, like all the tea being sweet and iced, or traffic stopping voluntarily for a funeral procession, or sneakers being called tennis shoes . . . I could go on and on.

Anyway, our yard had a bunch of screeching insects flying around, and a dog that loved to bite moving bugs.

Snowman totally lost it.

He'd swallowed who knows how many cicadas when he started gagging. The coughing changed to wheezing. All of a sudden, the poor little dog was desperately sucking in air that had nowhere to go.

Lily dropped her prized seed pack and sprinted over, grabbed him up like a doll, and administered the Heimlich maneuver for babies. I know because I learned it when I took my Red Cross babysitting course, but I would never have thought of using it on a dog.

It worked!

Maybe it was a coincidence, and he would have coughed up

all those scratchy bugs blocking his throat anyway, but I have to give Lily credit for fast thinking.

She's clearly got potential, and I think I could be an awesome sister.

I could teach her tons. Like when I told her to water her seeds with the sprinkling can, not squirt them with the garden hose, or they'd wash away.

Or maybe I could talk her into wearing clothes that actually fit. Lily isn't really fat, but in my tight-fitting hand-me-down tops, she's shaped more like a grape than a girl. Her oversized T-shirts aren't much better. They make her look like an underage bag lady.

I wonder if she'd let me cut her hair.

Lily

My sunflower is the only thing that's mine.

Bubbles used to be mostly my cat, but now, because V likes to feed her, she hangs out with both of us. Which is okay, but that's not all.

I have to share my room with Parker. I have to share Parker with Eric.

And I have to share my Mom with everybody— Frank, Eric, V, Parker, five carpools, her computer customers, and every cashier at Bi-Lo.

Mom makes so many trips to the grocery store that they all know her by name and purchase profile. I bet she's the only customer in town who buys bread, milk, orange juice, six kinds of cereal, a gallon of ice cream, two bags of Doritos, and is right back in line four hours later because it all ran out.

"I can't seem to get the hang of feeding six people." She pushes her hair back, grabs her car keys, and bolts out the door . . . again.

Even my clothes used to be V's. The hand-me-down tops that she outgrew or, more likely, that went flying out of style about two seconds ago.

My friend Cassie claims this is a good thing.

"V has the coolest clothes on the planet," she says to me as we walk to English class.

"Look at me," I say, pulling down the hem of my shirt, hoping it will stay stretched.

Obediently, she checks me out.

"You look soooo good!" she shouts, emphasizing "soooo" by flinging her hands wildly into the air.

"Cassie," I say flatly, "my stomach is showing. On V, that is hot. On me, it is not."

"Well . . ." Cassie hesitates, clearly confounded by the undeniable truth I have just uttered. "You have great teeth."

I *do* have great teeth. Straight and white, not too big. They're my best feature. But a winning smile doesn't hide any of the leftover baby fat clinging to my short self.

"*I* am a baggy T-shirt person," I state. "Not a show-your-belly-button style-queen."

"Okay," she concedes, "so maybe it's not you. But I would love"—she flings her hands again—"to have her wardrobe."

"Wardrobe?" I shriek. "How old are you? Fifty? A hundred? Wardrobe?" I start laughing hysterically. "How about her garments? Would you like to have her garments?"

"Outfits!" she shouts at me, her face flushing deep red. "I'd love to have her *outfits*."

I stifle my giggles. Cassie and I cannot help that we are uncool. Besides, neither one of us has what it takes to wear V's clothes. Popularity, confidence, and amazing abs. That's what it takes.

Where V has sleek, Cassie and I have slump. But I don't tell her that.

After all, Cassie and my sunflower are the only two things I don't have to share with a million other people.

So, I try to remember to be extra nice to Cassie, and I water my sunflower every day.

V showed me how to plant it—where *she* wanted it to go. And she paid for the seed pack—$1.19 at Wal-Mart.

It's that kind of stuff that confuses me. Is she being a power freak . . . or helpful? Generous . . . or tricking me into owing her?

Either way, most of the seeds washed away because, when V wasn't there, I squirted them too hard with the hose.

One came up, though. And it's mine. A green shoot that pushed up through the earth, as thick as a broom handle and almost as sturdy. It's growing faster than Jack's beanstalk, and just as determined to reach the sky.

Parker

"The Spicewood Cafeteria!" Parker cried out enthusiastically. It was his favorite place to eat, and Frank had just asked everybody where they wanted to go for dinner.

V made a face like she'd swallowed a bee.

"Pizza Hut," suggested Lily.

"Mort's Deli," said Eric.

V put her face back together and said, "I could cook spaghetti here."

"We're eating out," said Eric in a voice that implied, *What're you? Stupid?*

"Fine," she muttered. "Then let's go to Vito's. We haven't had Italian in forever."

"Pizza Hut is Italian," said Lily.

"No, it's not," said V firmly. "Pizza was invented by Americans."

"Since whe—," Lily started to disagree, then stopped, sagged, and returned her attention to the word puzzle she'd been working at the kitchen table.

Parker was surprised that his sister shut up so easily. She never used to do that. Where was the Lily who played War and Slapjack with him and argued over every single rule like it mattered?

Who knows? At least she was still smart-Lily. He was forever amazed that his sister could do the daily jumble in the newspaper. He could do the kiddy one—the one with three- and four-letter words. But Lily solved the grown-up one, almost every day.

Before Mom had married Frank, Lily also made decisions about where they ate out, because just about anything was fine with Mom and Parker. And Lily had great ideas.

But tonight Parker had a preference.

"The Spicewood Cafeteria," he begged. "Please."

He wanted to ask Papa Bud about the cicadas. He'd been collecting dead ones in a shoebox. He'd seen billions more on the news though, covering up places like Washington, DC. Would Charlotte, North Carolina, get that many? Papa Bud would know.

And, he couldn't stop picturing the plates—fried chicken, Jell-O, strawberry shortcake—which he would slide out from under the protective glass as he pushed his tray down the line. He always picked the same food at the cafeteria. Since the Jell-O sat on a piece of lettuce and had canned peaches jelled into the middle, Mom let him count it as a fruit *and* a vegetable.

"Chicken Cacciatore," V tempted her dad. "With a side of spaghetti." Then she flashed her perfect smile at Mom and cooed, "Eggplant Parmesan. With a bruschetta appetizer. Come on, you guys have been counting carbs all week. Splurge!"

Mom smiled back. "I'm just happy we're all doing something together. You kids decide."

Was she loony? thought Parker. Was this the same mom who claimed he didn't pay attention! *Everybody* had made different choices. Four restaurants. How had she missed that?

There was only one way to decide. Parker shoved his balled-up fist toward Eric, who was leaning against the kitchen counter.

Eric straightened up and pushed his fist out to meet Parker's. They both pumped them up and down three times, then Eric ended with his palm open. Parker stopped with his index and middle finger extended out in a V.

Scissors cuts paper.

"I win!" shouted Parker. "That means Eric has to side with me."

"No way!" shrieked V.

Lily continued to work her puzzle.

"Let's vote," gloated Parker. "All in favor of the cafeteria . . ."

Parker and Eric raised their hands.

"I guess that's it then," acknowledged Frank, grabbing his car keys off the dragonfly hook by the door. "Let's go."

"Shotgun!" claimed Parker.

"Dream on," grumbled V.

"Not so fast, Mud Boy." Frank reached out and snagged him by the collar with his index finger. "Your mother has permanent privileges for riding shotgun. It was one of our wedding vows."

"Aw . . ."

"And go put on a clean shirt."

Parker looked down at his T-shirt. He knew it had a huge locomotive somewhere underneath the dirt and used to say "Tweetsie Railroad" before the "Tweet" part got ripped off. He'd spent most of the afternoon playing King of the Hill with five other boys on a gravel pile behind the Fishers' unfinished house.

He had lost twelve out of fourteen times.

"Way to go!" Eric had said when Parker told him about it. He'd held up his hand to high-five him.

"Huh?" Parker had returned the congratulating slap, but he didn't know why.

"Do the math a better way," Eric said.

"Huh?" Parker repeated.

"Mud Boy," said Eric. "Think. It means you won twice."

Parker bolted down the hall, happily remembering Eric's praise, and into the room he shared with Lily.

"Don't leave me," he shouted back over his shoulder.

Hurriedly, he riffled through the neat stack of laundry

that Mom had left on the bed for Lily and him to put away. An extra-large, super-old, Powerpuff Girls T-shirt, two much smaller jazzy pink and lavender tops, a bra. Well, Lily called it a bra, but it was so flat it didn't even have cups. It had puckers.

Maybe he was only nine, but he knew what a bra was supposed to look like. He'd seen one of Aunt May's hanging on a clothesline in back of her house, and it had cups so big eagles could have nested in them.

It was weird having girl stuff in his room.

Mom said it was only for two years, until Eric went away to college. Then everyone would have his own room. He didn't really mind, though. It meant he never had to be alone.

"Wait for me!" he yelled, pulling on his favorite shirt, the one with a triceratops's head wrapping around to the front. It was clean, except for a blueberry stain that would never come out.

He didn't know what the big deal was about the shirt he'd had on earlier, but if it meant he could eat at the cafeteria, changing clothes was worth the trouble.

As it turned out, it was worth it big time.

ERIC

Journal Entry #171

Rock-Paper-Scissors is a little kid's game with big adult potential.
What if world leaders made compromises that way?
Wouldn't that be better than no decision at all?

Parker

When they arrived at the cafeteria, Parker flung open the doors and ran straight toward Papa Bud.

"Parker!" exclaimed the old man. He was wearing a blue sport coat and a tie. He had white hair, cropped neat and short into a crew cut. "How's my—"

"My name's Mud Boy now," Parker interrupted, keeping his face serious so Papa Bud would know that what he'd just said was important.

"Mud Boy!" exclaimed the old man happily. "How's my little buddy today? Third grade treating you right?" He wrapped one large arm around Parker and squeezed.

Lily rushed up and slipped under his other arm. "Hi, Papa Bud!"

Frank slapped him on the back. Mom kissed his wrinkled cheek. Eric hung back with his hands stuffed in his pockets, acting interested in the pictures hanging in the lobby.

"You young'uns are a sight for old, sore eyes!" drawled Papa Bud.

"Shake his hand," Frank hissed toward Eric.

Eric stepped forward quickly, and stuck out his hand.

"Well, look at you! You've grown a foot," greeted Papa Bud, pumping Eric's hand like it was the best thing that had happened to him all day.

Of course, that's what Papa Bud did. He greeted people. The owners of the Spicewood Cafeteria actually paid him to do it. Parker thought it might be the coolest job on earth.

"They *pay* him to be friendly?" he'd asked his mom.

"It gives the place warmth," Mom had explained. "You know—he makes customers feel at home."

"And where's that pretty new niece of mine?" Papa Bud asked Mom.

Parker looked all around for V, then finally spotted her, already in the food line, reaching forward to pick up her tray.

Mom and Frank exchanged looks, as if they were both embarrassed about something. Parker glanced down to make sure that he really had changed his shirt. They weren't ashamed of his blueberry stain, were they?

"Papa Bud," said Parker, stuffing his shirttail into the front of his shorts. "What's the deal with all the cicadas?"

Parker listened to Papa Bud's answer while everybody else filed ahead to the food line.

By the time Parker caught up, everyone had gotten their food and found a table, except Frank, who was waiting by the cashier to pay for Parker's meal.

"Where's your vegetable?" said Frank.

Parker proudly pointed at his jiggling lime Jell-O.

"Just because it's green," said Frank gently, "doesn't mean it's a vegetable."

Parker pointed at the limp piece of lettuce under his square of Jell-O.

When Frank slipped into his seat at the table, he eyed Mom and said, "Jell-O? A vegetable?"

She shrugged and smiled. Which meant, *let it go, honey*. She picked up her fork and skimmed some coleslaw from her white, single-serving minibowl.

"I found out about the cicadas," Parker announced excitedly. "Only Papa Bud calls them July flies, and this year we have a lot, but nowhere near the billions and billions other places got, and we probably won't either, but it's called Brood X, and they only show up once every seventeen years, and if we want to get rid of the ones in our yard, he says we can eat them because they're high in protein, low in fat, and, guess what? No carbs."

Parker aimed this last bit of information at Mom and Frank. Then he gulped air to get his breath back.

"Gross," said V.

"Cool," whispered Eric, reaching his black-sleeved arm across the table to swipe one of Frank's French fries. "What do they taste like?"

"Nutty," said Parker.

Mom lowered her fork. "Sweetie," she said softly, "I think Papa Bud was pulling your leg."

"Nuh-uh." Parker shook his head firmly. "He has recipes."

"Right," said Mom, scooping up another bite of coleslaw. "Cicada soufflé with a side of fish scales."

Parker grinned. "Nuh-uh. Monkey brains."

"Eye of newt," said Eric.

"Dragon tails," added Parker.

"Sasquatch fur," said Eric, laughing.

"Horse manure!" roared Parker, pounding the table.

"Stop them!" shouted V. "Before I throw up."

"Okay, boys," said Frank, eyeing Eric and laying special emphasis on the boys part, "that's enough."

"Let's talk about something nice," said Mom.

"My sunflower is about to bloom," said Lily. "It's grown so fast, the stalk is as tall as I am. And it has a bud—"

"What do ghosts spread on bagels?" asked Parker.

"Let Lily finish," scolded Frank.

"Scream cheese," Parker answered, pounding the table again.

Eric laughed. Everyone else groaned, except Lily, who said, "I can't wait to see what shade of yellow it is. The seed packet says it's—"

"What did the nut say when it sneezed?" interrupted Eric.

"Cashew!" exclaimed Parker.

Even V and Mom laughed out loud.

This is so fun, thought Parker. Having a big family is awesome.

Frank laughed, too, but then he stopped and shot a wicked look at Eric. Next, he turned to Lily and said, "Sorry, Princess. What were you saying?"

"Lemon Leopold. That's the color on the pack—"

"Princess!" V practically spit the word onto the table along with the pieces of cornbread she was chewing.

Lily blushed.

Frank looked confused, then guilty.

Everyone stared down at their plates. Even Parker knew that "Princess" was what Frank called V. It would be like Eric calling someone else Mud Boy. That was *his* name.

"Well," said Frank, reaching over and squeezing V's arm. "I guess you're both my princesses now. Aren't I the lucky one?"

"Yes, honey. You are," said Mom, her voice a nervous quiver. Then she turned to Lily. "What were you saying, honey?"

"Nothing," answered Lily quietly.

"Well, then," Mom chirped, still sounding weird. "What's up with you, Eric?"

Eric stared blankly at her for a minute. Then he brightened and sat up straighter in his chair. "Guess what kind of car I want," he said.

"A car?" asked Frank. "Who says you're getting a car?"

Eric glared at his dad. "Not now. When I'm sixteen, Dad. In four months. Remember?"

"Of course I remember, but we haven't decided you can have a car. We need to talk about—"

"I've saved up my own money," said Eric flatly.

Frank sighed. "Son," he said seriously, "you worked hard

last summer. And I know it paid well, but a car costs a lot more than—"

"Yay!" shouted Parker. "What're you getting?" He was popping up and down like a Jack-in-the-box.

Eric turned to Parker and grinned. "A hearse," he said.

"A hearse!" they all exclaimed, so loud that a lady with chicken grease on her chin lowered her drumstick, turned, and looked at them from the next table over. Two kids at the table to their right stared. Their parents cut their eyes away, but leaned left, obviously hoping to hear more—maybe about dead people or something.

"I've located a silver 1981 Buick Electra conversion," Eric said calmly, aiming this fantastic news directly at Parker. "It's by Armbruster/Stageway. Twenty feet long. V-eight engine. Sells for a mere $650.00."

Eric crossed his arms over the dried-up face of some bearded old-guy on the front of his black T-shirt, and leaned back in his chair. "Sweet," he added.

Parker thought it was about the best news he'd ever heard. His brother was going to drive a hearse. His friends would be jealous. No. They'd be excited. Just think of the car-pool possibilities.

Parker had always loved the Spicewood Cafeteria, but tonight was the best ever. He got to eat not one, but two strawberry shortcakes and a piece of apple pie because Lily, Frank, and V had all lost their appetites.

If the Spicewood Cafeteria were a body part, it would be an armpit.

The lobby has frumpy faded furniture with framed pink sunsets hanging above them that look as though they came straight off the bargain aisle at Kmart.

And the smell! Gobs and gobs of overcooked food. Old people scarfing it down like candy. The green beans are cooked away to mush with disgusting pieces of fat mixed in with them.

Mary Beth said, "Relax, that's just ham hock."

Ham *what*!? It sounded to me like a piece of pig somebody threw up.

This town is so weird. One night we go to a sushi bar and get scrumptious delicacies, then the next week to a fifties diner with gross brown gravy dumped over something called country-style steak. Only it doesn't look like any steak I've ever seen. It's dark mystery meat that bears a scary resemblance to cottage cheese, dyed brown.

When we were living in Chicago, I couldn't imagine moving to North Carolina. Isn't that where they make those movies with poor people living in the mountains? The ones where everybody plays a banjo and nobody has any teeth. Don't they have dentists? Would everyone wear shoes?

I admit, I was worried. But then we moved into a nice house, on a pretty street, and the neighbors seemed normal enough. There were plenty of dentists and the phone book was big and fat—not like Chicago, but big enough. Uptown, it even has skyscrapers.

Good shops. Lots of cool clothes.

Two things are actually better than home. The growing season is longer, so Dad and I can plant more vegetables. And I made the soccer *and* the tennis teams, because this school is smaller.

But just when I thought everything here was normal, I stumble on a place like the Spicewood Cafeteria. The only things worth eating there are apple pie and cornbread. With butter, it's really good.

But the weirdest part is that they have a greeter. That's a man who says "Howdy" to everyone who walks through the door. He's an old man, always wearing the same baby blue polyester sport coat and too-yellow tie. Hair grows out of his ears and he calls everyone under thirty "young'un."

The worst part is, I'm related to him! He's Parker and Lily's great uncle, and therefore—*my* great uncle.

His backyard has a clothesline in it.

With underwear flapping in the breeze.

Where anyone can see it.

Not that many people do. He lives in an old white farmhouse way outside the city—between Mint Hill and Locust. You have to drive on a dirt road to get to it. Dusty jars of homemade jam line his kitchen counter, and his nearest neighbor is a half mile away.

When his wife died last year, he was so lonely, he got a job being friendly to strangers. I'm trying not to be a snob, but honestly, the whole idea gives me the creeps. The job *and* the underwear.

So, I have two great uncles now. One in North Carolina, and one in Ohio whom I never see.

And Dad has two princesses.

Lily

"Where *is* my fiery Lily?" says Mom, standing in front of the kitchen sink and smoothing my hair with one hand and tilting my chin up with the other.

I wish I knew.

Parker runs through the room bouncing a basketball.

"Not in the house!" shouts Mom, still stroking my head. I wish my hair worked like hers does. She can twist it up or wear it down, and she always looks good.

I soak up the soft touch of her long, thin fingers. They're graceful—not like my stubby ones.

"My willy-nilly Tiger Lily," she says.

"Don't call me that in front of V or Eric," I beg.

"My little go-getter," she continues, as though I hadn't even spoken. "The girl with so many projects, so many opinions."

Gone, I think. Buried. Six feet under bossy V and abnormal Eric.

All my opinions get shot down. *Ka-pow!*

By V. Her Majesty Miss Know-Absolutely-Everything. But she doesn't know everything. Until she moved here, she'd never even seen a dirt road. And ha! It just so happens, pizza *is* Italian. I looked it up on the Internet.

And projects? I try to think of some of my old ones. Like scrapbooking all of Mom's photographs. I organized a July Fourth parade once, and wrote a neighborhood newspaper. For three whole months I fed an injured baby squirrel with an eyedropper and learned a ton about how to release animals back into the wild. Last year Cassie and I put on an awesome mystery play for Parker and his friends. We painted a backdrop for it using ideas from the board game Clue. Professor Plum, in the ballroom, with a dagger.

Only now, I know Eric could act out something ten times darker and creepier that Parker would like fifty times better. And V would have a hundred reasons why we should all do it some other way.

Mom wraps her arms around me and pulls me close.

I hug her back. She feels tense, and the usual padding on her bones is missing. Has she lost weight?

"I wish I knew where my days go," said Mom with a sigh. "If only I had more time. With you. With everybody." Wearily, she drops her arms, then pushes her hair back. "Maybe you and I could plan something fun. And V. I bet she'd love—"

"Actually," I remind Mom, "I do have a project."

Her eyes light up.

"A sunflower," I say.

Mom's shoulders relax, as though somebody just cut a rope that'd been holding them stiff.

"Of course," she says. "You told us about it at dinner last week. Has the bud opened yet?"

"Yes!" I shout. "And Mom, it's beautiful. Can you believe it grew so fast? Come see!" I tug on her arm.

"Oh, sweetie," she slumps. "Not now. I've got to start dinner. Later, though." She gives my shoulders a love-you squeeze, scoops a vegetable peeler off the kitchen counter, and scurries off toward the potato bin.

Wham! The back door.

Eric is home.

I ease out of the kitchen, down the hall, through the front door, and into the yard. I walk around back to the garden to water my sunflower, which doesn't need watering because I soaked it an hour ago.

I'm not in the mood for Eric. Sometimes he scares me.

I mean, he wants to buy a hearse!

And everything he owns is black. Shoes, shirts, toothbrush. Where does he find a drugstore that carries black toothbrushes? CVS Gothic?

A tiny jolt tweaks my brain. Before I had an older brother and sister, I'd never even heard of Gothic. Am I turning cooler?

Probably not.

Is Eric cool? Or just weird?

He hardly ever smiles, and he takes showers so hot that the bathroom curtains wilt and so long that he's late for dinner.

Mom would never let me do that.

He doesn't have friends—at least none that I've ever seen. Unless you count three smelly guys who were here about six months ago. They haven't been around since, which is fine with me, because they filled our whole den up with hairy legs, evil laughs, and B.O.

But the most wacko thing about Eric is that he reads while he walks. No kidding. He ambles into the house reading, opens the refrigerator reading, wanders down the hall reading. He even takes out the trash reading.

How does he do that? Without running into a wall, I mean.

Why would he even *want* to do that?

And, he's so old, he shaves—once a week, because Frank makes him do it. The rest of the time he grows gross scratchy stubble on his chin and looks like a convict.

I whisper, "Hi," looking up and searching for my sunflower blossom. I notice that V has left her cicada-clearing rake leaning beside my plant.

My flower.

Then I see it.

Hanging. Broken. Dangling like a dead face from its tall, thick stalk.

ERIC

Journal Entry #172

Tolstoy's "Master and Man" is an awesome short story, but reading it makes me deep-down cold—the kind of iciness that only a long, hot shower can fix.

Does it ever get warm in Russia?

One guy had icicles hanging off his nostrils and hoarfrost all over his eyeballs. He was dead. The lucky guy with him—lucky because he didn't die—had to have three toes whacked off after they froze solid.

How important are toes? Not as bad as losing your eyes or an arm, but still . . .

If I lost three toes would I walk funny?

Would girls go out with me? They don't notice me now with toes.

I bet they'd notice if I drove a hearse.

Will Dad let me buy one?

Does he think I'm still a stupid kid because I goof around with Parker? Like the baby boy who named his new puppy Snowman 11 years ago?

What would I name him now? Something tough. Rambo? That sounds nothing like a slightly chubby white dog.

Yeti?

Hoarfrost?

What the heck is hoarfrost anyway?

Breaking News: Journal Entry #173

V smashed Lily's sunflower. Wham. Just like that. Instant compost.

My sister.

Why would she do that?

Because Dad has two princesses?

Maybe that hurt her pretty bad, but still. Killing that flower was almost murder.

Lily was quiet before. Now she's totally soundless.

And everybody else is screaming.

Dad to V: You're grounded!

V to Dad: I swear—I didn't do it!

Mud Boy to Lily: Come on. It's just a flower. Please, talk to us!

Dad to V: Don't lie to me!

Mary Beth to Mud Boy: Don't shout at your sister!

They're still yelling.

Snowman's barking.

So loud I can't read.

So. I'll keep writing.

What's left to say?

Lily. I feel rotten for her. She took care of that sunflower like it was her own kid.

But, at least it made Dad forget everything that's wrong with me. For now.

Journal Entry #174

"The mention of bad-tempered and unstable people reminds me that during the whole of this day my behavior has been above reproach."—*Dostoevsky, White Nights*

Lily

For one whole day, I do nothing. I say nothing. I feel so hollow. So cheated.

Get a grip, I tell myself.

I hear Parker pleading, *Lily, it's just a flower.*

He's right.

I'm numb over losing a stupid flower. I can't imagine what Eric and V must have felt like when their brother died. Parker said Eric told him that Ben was scary sick for a whole year.

At least he wasn't killed. Hacked down in broad daylight by his own sister.

I know she did it. I mean, come on—she actually left the murder weapon at the scene of the crime.

When I watered my sunflower, there was no rake. When I went back an hour later, V's rake was right there. Practically touching my plant—what was left of it.

I'm not numb anymore, though.

I'm mad.

I spot Frank's spray bottle full of Roundup, the one he uses to kill weeds deader than a stomped-on ant.

Roundup doesn't just wipe out weeds. It kills *all* plants.

Why did V kill mine?

Because her dad likes me?

What kind of a reason is that? Doesn't *my* mom like *her*? Well, I'm sure she would if she had time.

But do you see me chopping up her new clothes?

No.

I pick up the Roundup.

I stare at V's tomato project—the one that's going to bring her a pile of money. For what? More lip gloss? A new Victoria's Secret thong?

I squirt it harmlessly at the gravel path. Cicadas scurry in ten directions. Does Roundup kill bugs, too?

It's an awesome day. Blue sky, gentle breeze, fluffy white clouds. Not too hot. It makes me angry that I'm wasting all this time being angry.

I aim the Roundup at V's tomato plants. Should I zap them?

Of course not. I'm not mean like her.

I place the spray bottle back on the ground where I found it.

Will we ever get along?

I remember the day, a month after Mom and Frank got married—the day I thought V and I would be best friends.

Mom had left the house to call on one of her

computer customers. She does custom work and tutoring in other people's homes—installing new software, fixing glitches, teaching slick cyber tricks. All the stuff that old people over forty with home computers need. Only they have to find someone like her who speaks non-tech language, slow and simple.

Frank, Eric, V, Parker. All gone. I had the house totally to myself.

I outgrew dolls a long time ago. But sometimes, if I'm home sick and no one is watching, I get out my Barbies. I don't know why. It's just fun.

I never ever did the Barbie-loves-Ken stuff, or blushing-bride-Barbie, or just-got-her-nails-done Barbie.

Gag.

No. My Barbies are damsels in distress. Locked in tall chest-of-drawer towers, waiting to be rescued by Parker's G.I. Joes.

Or I make them be Kung-Fu Barbies, flipping through the air and kicking Darth Vader's storm troopers into cyberspace.

But when Mom married Frank, it seemed too risky, so I packed them all up and hid them in the attic.

One day, I sneaked back up and pulled them all out. Everything. Even the Barbie Jammin' in Jamaica Buggy and the entire Cali Girl Beach Pool Playset. Half my room was morphed into a pink-and-purple wonderland. Plastic stuff everywhere. Parker's bed was the evil kingdom of Garlic Breath, and his Incredible Hulk had trapped Barbie in a black cave under the pillow where she was suffocating because of bad air.

"Barbie?" said V in a voice of total astonishment. "You're playing with Barbie?"

I whirled around to see V standing in my doorway, eyes wide, a smile playing at the corners of her mouth.

"No," I said, feeling the heat rise up around the collar of my shirt and explode onto my face.

Of course I was playing with Barbie. Any fool could see that I was playing with Barbie. There was no made-up explanation on earth that would make a sliver of sense. So I just said *no*.

Let her deal with the absurdity of it all. *No* was my final answer.

She stood there looking snobby for about a minute, then she scanned the hall for witnesses. Next she picked up one of Parker's X-wing fighter jets and flew it in to rescue blue-in-the-face Barbie, who was gasping her last.

She plopped down beside me on the floor, scooped up three skimpy doll outfits and folded them into a piece of Barbie's matching airport luggage. She tossed the whole thing, along with Barbie's boom box, into the back of a Corvette.

"Here," she said, thrusting Barbie's Princess Horse Marzipan and Luke Skywalker at me. "Saddle them up and meet me in Venezuela before sunset."

It took me a minute to process the shock. Then I fell backward onto the floor, laughing so hard I thought I would cry.

We played goofball Barbie for an hour. Nutty stuff. Wild and crazy. I loved my new sister.

Two days later, Cassie and I were watching TV in the den when V strolled through with her new friend, Jessica. Jessica is the type of person who goes to the pool every day of her life, but has never gotten wet.

Cassie thinks she's interesting.

I think she's more boring than a spit-out wad of chewing gum, but I say, "Hi, Jessica," just to be friendly.

"That's Lily," says V, her chin up in the air. "She still plays with dolls."

It's almost a year later, but thinking about it, even now, makes my heart cramp up as if a huge hand had just squeezed it like a lemon. The same feeling I get when I look at my broken sunflower stalk. The one that's turning brown from the top down.

I pick up the bottle of Roundup and squirt a dozen of V's tomato plants before I can stop myself.

But I do stop. I can't make myself destroy her entire project, even if she deserves it.

It doesn't matter, though. The breeze carries all the poison to all fifty plants.

I didn't know it would do that.

Parker

I didn't know it would do that, thought Parker, staring miserably at the scuffed-up basketball in his grimy hands.

Who knew it would bounce so high? Or hit so hard?

He dropped the ball and watched it roll to the end of the driveway. Then he ran as fast as he could toward it, kicking it so hard it stung his toes like a hornet.

"Stupid ball!" he shouted after it as it soared across the street, bounced against the curb, then spun all the way to the storm drain in front of the Flannigans' house.

Good, he thought.

He hoped it got sucked down a pipe and into the Atlantic Ocean.

Parker swiped angrily at a tear with his dirty fingers, streaking his face with mud.

"Stupid, stupid ball," he repeated. "You made me break Lily's flower."

V

After school, Mary Beth dropped me off at the end of our driveway so I could roll our empty trashcan back to the garage. At least she thinks I can do *something*.

I can't wait until Eric gets his license. Then he can drive us all home from school. The ride home today was beyond boring.

Parker, who's usually louder than the cicadas, was mute as a brick. Lily sat in the front seat and moved her head in different directions every time her mom asked her a question.

"Are you all right?"

Nod.

"Anything wrong?"

Shake.

"You're so quiet."

Shrug.

"Is this about your flower?"

Violent shake.

To her credit, Mary Beth had whispered the last question— so she wouldn't make me, the sunflower slayer, uncomfortable. But I heard her anyway.

All of them think I murdered Lily's precious plant, but I didn't.

Eric read his fat book all the way home. Why doesn't that make him carsick?

Personally, I was thrilled to get to escape the car eight seconds early, even if it was to retrieve a garbage can. Mary Beth probably thought I'd love that job since it meant I could squash innocent bugs on the way down the driveway—killer that I am.

I felt terrible for Lily. She loved that plant. But I couldn't figure out how to tell her without it sounding like a confession. *I'm sorry*, implies *sorry because I killed it*.

How *did* it die?

I searched and searched for clues, but there weren't any signs of disease or bugs or weed killers. It just looked broken, as if someone had clubbed it with a baseball bat. Or my rake.

I waited until I heard the back door slam, meaning everyone had filed into the house like zombies. I pictured Eric, still reading his book. How did he walk and read at the same time?

Vroom! Mary Beth had not gone in the house. She'd reversed the car and was backing out of the driveway—zipping off to somewhere.

I waved, trying to stop her and ask if I could do anything to start dinner. She waved back and kept going. *Clueless* does not begin to describe this woman.

I opened the door to Dad's tool room, searching for my rake. Was it still in the garden? Yuck. How many cicadas would I have to step on to get to my tomato plants?

I pictured how green and beautiful they were—ready to sell.

I wondered if Parker would let me borrow his wagon to take them door-to-door. Or should I go to each house with only five or six placed neatly in a box?

And what should I say first?

Would you like to buy some tomato plants?

Or, *I'm raising money to buy soccer balls for children in Iraq?*

No. The first thing I should make perfectly clear, before they pinched up their faces thinking about digging in the dirt and sweating, was *I'll plant them.*

Then I could explain that the soil in our neighborhood tended to have the perfect pH—slightly acid—for tomatoes. I'd offer to sprinkle some cottonseed meal in for free, and then describe how I would bury a few of the lower shoots so that they would root too, giving the plant extra ways to suck up water in case of drought.

All the neighbors would think I was a total plant genius. Last, I'd mention the soccer balls. A generous genius, they'd think, and happily buy three plants, maybe four.

I edged around the corner of the house and into the garden, tiptoeing around the bugs.

When I looked up, I saw drooping weeds where my plants should be.

My plants were gone.

No. I looked again. Not gone. The ugly weeds *were* my tomatoes.

I couldn't believe what my eyes were telling me.

Fifty plants. All limp. Sick. Brown. Dying.

No. I inched closer. Not dying.

Dead.

Lily

I'm sitting in my room, wishing I were dead, when V explodes through the door like a bomb.

"You disgusting, vicious little creep!" she screams. "You killed my plants!"

Her face is as red as her tomatoes would have been.

"I hate you!" she keeps yelling. "I didn't kill your stupid plant!"

I've known all day that this was coming. But I still don't have a clue what to say.

I only meant to kill a few?

I'm only a partly disgusting, vicious little creep?

I wonder how she knew I did it, but I'm not surprised. V is a super-sleuth genius when it comes to plants. Maybe I left fingerprints on the Roundup, or Lily-breath on the shriveled up leaves.

"I'm sorry," I whisper, knowing it's not good enough.

"Sorry?!" she shrieks. She takes a giant step toward me and I shrink. What if she decides to hit me?

"You'll *be* sorry," she shouts. She turns and storms out of the room, slamming the door behind her.

Parker's Shrek poster slides to one side. The big green ogre, with that goofy air of goodness he has plastered all over him, is looking at me sort of lopsided.

You, I say to him, are only ugly on the outside. I am ugly everywhere.

No.

Wait.

I didn't *mean* to kill them all.

Besides, look what *she* did!

Aren't we even?

ERIC

Journal Entry #174

"He was an old man who fished alone in a skiff in the Gulf Stream and he had gone eighty-four days now without taking a fish."—*first sentence of* The Old Man and the Sea, *by Ernest Hemingway*

I'm sick of Russia. All those wars and hoarfrost made me tired and cold. Suddenly everything about it reminded me of home. Dostoevsky writing about why people act the wacko way they do—Tolstoy writing about wars and family problems. So I asked Mr. Jackman what I could read that wasn't about families or fighting—something tough, man against nature. How about Moby Dick?

Eric, he says, you amaze me. But give it a rest, man. Moby Dick *is a thousand pages. Treat yourself to something short.*

The Old Man and the Sea, *he says.*

I like long books—getting lost in them for weeks.

The Hemingway book is so short it feels like Cliff's Notes. But it's cool. The language is lean and hard.

There's a boy in it who wants to help this old guy catch fish, but his dad won't let him, because the old man is a loser. He hasn't caught a fish in 84 days.

"I am a boy and I must obey him," says the kid, but he still wants to do something nice for the old man, so he buys him a drink, and the wrinkled, leathery old fisherman calls him a man.

I know I should help out with our family crisis. Lily and V hate each other. Dad and Mary Beth are big-time stressed about it. Even Mud Boy is acting psycho.

Dostoevsky would figure them all out in a heartbeat.

I'd rather read.

Lily

V and I are both grounded. Stuck at home. Together.

It's so unfair. Not the part about being grounded—we both deserve that. But being alone with her in this house feels like I'm a lamb locked up with a lion. Well, maybe not a lamb. More like a rat. Either way, I hide quietly in the corners of our big cage and hope she doesn't smell me.

I can hear her banging around in the kitchen. And vacuuming the den. Is she bored, or just so mean that she's trying to keep me out of the best rooms?

What I *should* do is my history homework—that and dream up a science topic. School will be out in a month, and Mrs. Finley wants a science project!

Talk about mean.

She thinks we need something serious to keep us from quitting too early.

It doesn't matter though, because I can't concentrate on anything except the bad vibes in this house. I swear, I can actually feel them. On my skin. Like a pulse.

So I lay low, think about how my diseased science

grade is about to get sicker, and work a lot of word puzzles.

I'm sprawled across my bed staring at "almbe" and trying to unscramble it. Usually the five-letter words are a cinch. It's the six-letter words that cramp my brain. But I can't think about anything but Mom and Frank, who slipped into my room a while ago, like ghosts, easing onto Parker's squeaky bed.

"Lily," said Mom, holding Frank's hand for support. "You and V need to apologize to each other."

Frank sat straight up, looking super confident, as if that would fix everything.

"I already did," I said. "First thing. I told her I was sorry. But she was madder than anything—ever. Not that I blame her. So, I tried again later. When she was calmer."

"What did she say then?" asked Mom.

Frank leaned forward, hopeful.

I eyed him carefully. Should I repeat the exact words his daughter said? No way. My second apology had made her even madder than the first one. The stuff she'd said would get me grounded for life.

"She told me to go pretty far away," I reworded.

Frank cringed.

"Anything else?" he asked.

"She swore she never touched my gall-darned sunflower."

His shoulders sagged.

"And?" Mom dug some more.

"That's about it," I lied. Why bother with the part where V claimed she planned to spend her tomato profits on soccer balls for kids in Iraq? I mean, give me a break. Soccer balls? Iraq?

And I'm going to send my bread crusts to starving children in Africa.

Frank and Mom left the room looking about a ton heavier than when they glided in.

I bet they know V didn't say "gall-darned." I don't even say "gall-darned." But I've heard Papa Bud say it a million times, and it seemed a fair enough way to rephrase what she really said.

Papa Bud has an old-timey way of talking that sometimes says things better than Shakespeare could've.

Right now he would say that I am in a world of hurt.

He would also tell me to forgive V because the Bible says so.

I know that, because I go to Sunday school. V and Eric probably don't know that, because they hardly ever go. Mom says I have to, but V and Eric are old enough to decide for themselves.

That is so not fair.

I go back to solving my puzzle.

I could feel the tension in this house. Actually *feel* it. When Dad and Mary Beth came into my room for the big talk, I swear, the air around my skin got heavier and vibrated.

I acted busy, doing algebra homework at my desk. They eased themselves onto the end of my bed as though it might break. Mary Beth gave Dad's arm a gentle squeeze of support that I wasn't supposed to see. It wouldn't have surprised me if she'd said a prayer. *Please God, be with Frank in this moment of crisis, and forgive V her sins. Amen.*

"V," said Dad. "You and Lily need to apologize to each other."

"No way," I said, not looking up from my equation.

"She apologized to you," said Mary Beth gently.

"Ha!" I answered.

"*Ha?*" asked Dad, irritation edging into his voice. "What's 'Ha!' supposed to mean?"

"It means she *should* apologize to me," I said. "She killed fifty plants. She should pay me."

Dad sighed. "V, you killed *her* plant, too."

I flung down my pencil. "I did *not* kill her plant!" Tears of frustration welled up, stinging my eyes.

Why wouldn't anyone believe me?

"V," said Dad, rising up in anger. "You will stay grounded until you apologize to Lily."

He stalked out of the room, Mary Beth slinking behind him. She reached out to touch me as she went by, gently, on the tip of my shoulder.

So what? Who needs them?

They sure as heck didn't need me. Mary Beth treats me like a five-year-old. Helpless. While she—Wonder Woman—works, cooks, cleans, shops—and doesn't even know that I can help. That I *like* to help.

I used to do household stuff for Dad every day.

As soon as they left the house, I went to the kitchen and cleaned out a cabinet. Mary Beth had pots and pans stacked all over each other. Every time you opened the door to get a bowl or a saucepan, lids fell on the floor. I rearranged the whole mess. Slamming pots into new places. Lids on a separate shelf, stacked by size. I even sponged off the shelves, wiping away a year's worth of little spills. The organizing made me feel better, but the banging was the best part.

Then I dusted and vacuumed the den. She should pay me.

Maybe I could raise money that way. No way would I tell them my soccer ball plan. Who'd believe me?

They'd been so quick to think I'd lied about Lily's flower. *But why?* Am I so bad? I guided the vacuum behind the sofa and tried to think back. Well, maybe there was one time I acted sort of crummy. Or two . . .

Eric clomped into the den as I shut off the vacuum. He

glanced up from a skinny book he was reading. "Did Mary Beth ask you to clean up in here?"

"Nope," I said, picking up the feather duster.

"Are you crazy?" he asked.

"Nope," I answered, swiping his face with it.

"Gross, V." He windmilled his arms at me. "Knock it off." He wrinkled his nose into a twist, then sneezed.

"Guess what?" he said, wiping his nose on the sleeve of his T-shirt.

Maybe that's why he likes black clothes, I thought.

"I've been researching Rock-Paper-Scissors on the Internet," he continued.

"Rock-Paper-Scissors?" I repeated. What was he talking about?

"Yeah," he said. "You know—the hand game Mud Boy and I've been using to make decisions around here. And guess what?"

"What?" I said, wondering if he'd really finally lost it. Reverted all the way back to age five—the age that Mary Beth thought I was.

"It's a big-time game. Adults play it. They have tournaments. Strategies. It's bigger than chess." He glowed like a little kid with a brand-new dirt bike.

"Bigger than chess?" I repeated.

"Well," he said, twisting his shirt, "maybe not bigger than chess. But big."

"Whatever," I mumbled, picking up a lamp and dusting under it.

"Man, V," he grumbled, then muttered a bunch of stuff that I couldn't hear as he huffed out of the room and down the hall.

Maybe Dad was right to worry about him. I stopped dusting. *Did* Dad worry about him? Sometimes, when Eric and Parker acted super goofy, he definitely seemed irritated, but other times I wondered if Eric didn't make a big deal out of nothing.

I pictured Ben—before he died. How old had he been? Fourteen. A whole year younger than Eric is now. Wow. Ben had sure acted a lot older. Or did Eric just seem younger? Except for the old and boring books he read. But hadn't I just seen him reading a really short book? What was it? I wondered. *Rock-Paper-Scissors? Goodnight Moon?*

I looked up and saw Lily standing in the doorway. Why wasn't she cowering and slinking past me like she usually did? Instead, she was gaping at me like a person who didn't believe in fairies, and then suddenly saw one in the flesh—real, after all.

"You had a phone call," she said, her voice higher than normal, and squeaky.

"When?" I asked. I hadn't heard it ring.

"Just now," she answered. "I guess you didn't hear it over the vacuum. And you didn't answer me when I yelled, so I took a message."

"Yeah?" I said. Why was she looking at me so funny? Had someone else in my family died?

"It was the manager of The Sport Shop," she said, her eyes wide. "He said to tell you that he can get you a discount on the soccer balls."

Parker

Parker tiptoed past V's door on his way down the hall.

Frank's voice coming from her room stopped him dead. "V," he said. "You killed *her* plant, too."

Parker flattened himself against the wall beside the door.

"I did *not* kill her plant!" screamed V.

Parker felt himself growing hot all over. Suddenly the air seemed so heavy he could barely breathe it.

"V," growled Frank, "you will stay grounded until you apologize to Lily."

Parker bolted down the hall to his room and slammed the door. His Shrek poster slid left.

"Could you *be* any noisier?" said Lily, who was sprawled across her bed working the daily word jumble.

Parker, his eyes stinging with tears, disappeared into his closet, frantically pretending to search through a stack of comic books in the corner. No way did he want Lily to see him cry.

The hall phone rang.

"I'll get it," mumbled Lily.

Parker backed out of his closet and flung himself onto

his bed. He jerked his pillow out from under the spread, buried his head under the dinosaur pillowcase, and tried not to cry.

What do I do? Lily will kill me. V's scary. What will she do? Will Eric hate me? What about Frank? I have to tell somebody what I did. No. I don't. Lily can grow another flower. Can't she? It was an accident! V won't stay grounded forever. Will she? No way. I wouldn't. I'd apologize. Even if I didn't do it.

But I did do it.

Out of nowhere, he pictured Mr. Fitch, his Sunday school teacher, jerking his head in that weird way that made everyone call him "Mr. Twitch." "The honest way is the only way—even if it hurts," he preached. *Twitch. Twitch.*

Easy for him to say, thought Parker, uncovering his head and turning over. He wiped his eyes dry with the back of his hand.

Besides, it's not like I lied. Nobody's asked.

Shrek hung lopsided on the wall, smiling down at him.

"What would you do?" Parker asked the ogre.

Shrek didn't answer.

Parker got up, pulled a tissue out of Lily's Kleenex box, and blew his nose. He inched to the door to see if Lily was coming back. Eric cruised past muttering, "Man, V. Have you ever turned into a crab. At least I've got a brother that's cool."

Neat-o, thought Parker, stepping back from the door and breaking into a grin.

Then he froze.

What would happen when Eric found out that he wasn't cool? That he was a criminal.

ERIC

Journal Entry #175

"Remember as far as anyone knows, we're a nice normal family."—*Homer Simpson*

Journal Entry #176

The Old Man and the Sea *is incredible. The fisherman fights this monster fish—a record marlin that weighs over 1,500 pounds. He fights it for days. Alone. But he wishes the boy were with him.*

The old man has dignity. So does the fish.

And my family is falling apart over a flower.

Parker

"Kids!" Frank shouted from the hall. "Everybody in the den. Now."

Uh, oh, thought Parker. He knew the voice of doom when he heard it. He wiped his eyes one more time with his fists and wondered if they were red. He hoped not.

When he got to the den, V and Lily were already there. V stood glaring at Lily with her chin stuck out and her hands on her hips as if her whole body was shouting, *I told you so!* Lily slumped lower than Snowman when he gets caught chewing somebody's shoe.

But when Frank strolled in, they both zapped their posture back to normal.

"Who . . ." Frank hesitated to add suspense. ". . . wants to go to a movie?"

Parker kept his face lowered. Then it hit him. A movie. They were going to a movie! "*Shrek 2!*" he shrieked.

"Let's go see *Troy*," said Eric.

"How about *Harry Potter*?" suggested Mom.

"How about we all go to a different one?" said Eric.

Parker saw Frank cut his eyes toward Eric in a kidding way that said, *you are no help*.

But Eric clenched his jaw muscles as if Frank's look had said, *shut up, dummy*.

Lily and V stood quietly invisible, probably hoping no one would remember they were grounded.

"V," said Frank, trading a weird glance with Mom, "we want you and Lily to go with us, but after that, you're back to grounded." He threw his arms wide. "So! What's it going to be?"

Parker thrust his fist toward Eric and started the Rock-Paper-Scissors countdown.

"Whoa," said Mom. "What about my suggestion?"

Parker and Eric looked at each other and nodded. "Three way," they agreed.

Mom pushed her hand into the circle. *Pump, pump, pump*.

Mom's fist ended on rock. Eric's and Parker's on paper.

"You're out, Mom."

Pump, pump, pump.

Parker was rock. Eric, scissors.

"*Shrek 2*, here we come!" Parker gloated. Then he got calm and asked, "Okay, Lily? Okay, V?"

They both shrugged and nodded.

Parker felt heat creeping up the back of his neck. Why couldn't they get over it? Were they going to dump guilt on him forever?

●

On the way into the movie, Eric and V acted as if they didn't know Mom, Frank, or anybody. But afterward, everyone walked out together, smiling. Even Lily looked happy.

It had rained while they were in the theater, but now the sun was out again, making the wet parking lot feel steamy.

Frank started quizzing everybody the second he cranked up the engine of the minivan.

"V," he asked cheerfully, "who was your favorite character?"

"Dad," V groaned, sinking lower in the backseat.

"Puss In Boots," offered Eric.

"Hey! Me too," said Lily, perking up and sounding surprised that she and Eric liked the same guy.

"Me three," said Parker. "He was so funny."

"And cute," added Lily.

"Cute!" Eric blurted. "He was an assassin!"

"What's an assassin?" asked Parker.

"A paid killer," answered Eric.

"A painkiller?" Parker asked.

"No," Eric chuckled. "*Paid*—emphasis on the d."

"Oh," said Parker, understanding. Then he laughed at himself and said, "Painkiller. Ha." He grinned. "Eric's favorite character is an aspirin."

Everybody laughed.

Parker beamed. He loved it when everyone thought he was funny.

Then Mom jumped in and said Shrek was her favorite. Frank liked Donkey, and V claimed she loved the hateful fairy godmother. Maybe she did.

"The giant Gingerbread Man was the best," said Parker.

"You already voted," said Lily, pushing him with her elbow.

Parker sank back in his seat, happy to hear her complain.

"Yeah," said Eric. "He got healed since the last movie—by yeast cell research."

Frank tossed his head back and laughed. "I missed that line."

Parker announced, "*Nobody* can catch the Gingerbread Man,"

"Okay," said Frank, still chuckling. You could tell he loved this. "Who knows what the moral was?"

"Dad," V groaned again.

"Well." Mom cleared her throat. "Shrek and Princess Fiona love each other—beautiful or ugly. So, it's about relationships, and the goodness inside people's hearts. . . ."

"Mom," groaned Lily.

Yay! thought Parker. He was glad Lily's old self was making a comeback. Besides, he'd wished Shrek and Fiona had stayed good-looking. Even if that wouldn't have been the best ending, he liked it anyway.

"Come on, guys," said Frank, trying to hide a goofball grin. "It's about a thoughtful dad who doesn't want his daughter to marry a big, green, swamp-dwelling monster. Who can blame him?"

"Frank," Mom moaned. She reached across the console and jokingly punched his arm.

Eric leaned forward, stroking the stubbly hairs on his chin as if he were a genius, and said, "It's about aging parents who worry unnecessarily about their kids."

"Aging?" Frank exclaimed, pretending to be mad. "You twerp."

"I thought it was romantic," said Lily.

"There's no such thing as Prince Charming," declared V.

"Did we see the same movie?" exclaimed Mom.

"V's right," agreed Lily, but then she crossed her arms and flopped back against her seat, "but it can *still* be romantic."

Yes! Parker cheered silently. Even if he thought that was a very dumb way of looking at a great movie, he was excited to see Lily let fly one of her kick-butt opinions again.

And what did *he* think it meant? He stared out the window as they cruised past the King of the Hill gravel pile, then turned onto the road their house was on. A woman in exercise shorts was walking fast along the wet sidewalk, pumping her arms. A gust of wind made the back of her T-shirt flap.

It had grown cloudy again, and dark. Like another storm coming. Parker looked up at all the tall oaks lining their street, and felt small.

He was pretty sure the movie meant that, big or little, you needed to do the right thing.

He was thankful no one had asked him.

Lily

I lie in bed with the lights out, trying to figure out what snapped in me today. Why do I feel more like myself—if only a little?

I picture the deck of cards with red and blue balloons all over it that Parker and I used to play games with. I was one of the cards on top. Then *boom*, somebody shuffled, and I ended up all the way at the bottom, a mile below V—the queen of diamonds. Barely above Parker, a jelly-smudged three of clubs.

I think that metaphor works, but I'll have to ask Eric. He agrees with me that the cat character in Shrek 2 is cool, so he can't be as scary as he looks.

I know I won't ever be the oldest again. And that's okay. But I'm not going to stay squashed at the bottom either.

I stare up at the ceiling and make some decisions.

One, it's time to reshuffle.

Two, V needs a serious attitude adjustment.

Okay, she did not lie about the soccer balls. That was the Surprise of the Month. But, once I thought about

it, it fit the good sister, the one who bought my sunflower seeds, played with Barbie, and talked me into
shaving my legs.

But she's lying about killing my sunflower—which
makes her the bad sister. The one who corrects everything I say, and shamed me in front of Jessica.

So here's the count as I see it: I have apologized to
her three times. Twice for zapping her plants. And once
for not believing her soccer-ball story.

"V," I told her, "I'm so sorry. You *were* raising money
for kids. Is it too late to plant more tomatoes? I'll pay for
the seeds. I'll help you plant them."

"You dummy," she sneered, with her hands on her
hips. "Of course it's too late. Don't you know anything?"

It's so not fair that she looks pretty, even when
she's not.

That's when Parker slunk into the room, trying to
hide his red eyes. What, I wonder, did V do to him?
And why has he been acting so quiet and un-Parker-like
lately?

Then Frank announced that we were all going on a
major peacekeeping mission to the movies. He and
Mom think they're so clever.

Come on. We're not stupid.

So. The apology score is Lily, 3. V, 0.

I haven't been counting all the things she's done to

me, but, if I had to come up with a number, I'd say she owes me about 736 *I'm sorrys*, not counting the sunflower murder.

I roll over and listen. Parker is one bed over, squirming, muttering, having a serious-sounding nightmare.

"It's okay," I say into the darkness.

But it's not okay, because he keeps twisting and murmuring, and won't wake up.

Earlier I tried to get him to play War, I Doubt It, Slapjack—anything so I could pry his problems out of him, and help.

"No thanks," he'd said.

No surprise there. He hasn't played cards with me since Eric became his favorite sibling.

"So what's wrong?" I asked when he got into bed.

"Nothing."

He reached up and switched off the light, and I hadn't even gotten into my pajamas yet.

"Parker," I said, turning the light back on. "Why were you crying this afternoon?"

"I wasn't crying!" he shouted at me, then covered his head with his pillow.

So now I'm listening to him, probably being attacked by a T. rex in his sleep. What does he expect when he sleeps on a pillowcase covered with dinosaurs baring a billion sharp teeth?

"Parker!" I shout. "Wake up! It's okay."

He snorts and sputters. I hear him sit up. "Wha—? Oh, thanks, Lily." Then he snuggles back into peaceful sleep.

This is my favorite time. When I feel alone and the room seems mine.

Tomorrow I start reshuffling.

I'm going to raise V's soccer-ball plan from the dead. Whether she likes it or not.

"Yikes!" exclaimed Mary Beth from the kitchen. "Who cleaned out my cabinet?"

Curled up on the sofa in the den, I smiled. Here it came. The awakening. Mary Beth opening her brain and realizing that an intelligent thirteen-year-old daughter came with the marriage.

"I did," I answered as casually as I could manage under the circumstances.

Mary Beth appeared in the doorway. "*You* did?"

Or, to be fair, maybe it was "You *did*?"

But I'm betting my money on the first one.

I waited for her to notice that the den had been dusted and vacuumed.

"V," she said warmly, "thank you so much. Imagine"—she turned and wandered back into the kitchen—"I can get out a pan now without an avalanche."

Silence. Then the sound of sizzling sausage drifted out, followed by the smell.

I felt half happy, half cheated.

"Did you notice the den?" I called after her.

"What, honey? I can't hear you over the sausage."

"The *den*!" I shouted.

"What men?" she shouted back.

I sighed, pushed myself up off the couch, and strolled into the kitchen.

"I vacuumed and dusted the den," I said.

Mary Beth flipped a sizzling patty, then lowered the spatula and stared at me through her hair straggles. She pushed them back with the back of her hand and said, "You did *what*?"

Emphasis definitely on *what*.

"Are you all right?" she asked, not even trying to hide her puzzled look. Hadn't Parker or Lily ever done anything around here besides make their beds and empty a wastebasket? They're not babies.

Are they?

"Do you have friends coming over?" she asked, as if that were the only answer that made sense.

"No," I said. "I just like to help out. You know, I helped Dad a lot."

Her blank face clearly stated that she didn't know. She followed it with a curious head tilt. Yes! I had her attention! Finally.

"What's for dinner?" I asked.

"Sausage biscuits and cheese omelets," she said, slowly turning over another hot patty. I watched the evidence of a useful V trying to force its way into her closed mind.

"Do we have any blueberries?" I asked.

Her head popped up so fast you'd think I'd said something weird, like *do we have any rare Egyptian pomegranates?*

"None fresh," she answered. "There's some frozen. I could go to the store."

"No!" I shouted. Then quieter, "Frozen are fine. I'll make dessert. Okay?"

She looked up at me with the same eyes that Lily had yesterday. Super-wide-open, staring at the fairy that no one believed in, but there she was. Real.

Me.

Parker

"This isn't about you, Parker," said Lily. "It's between V and me. We'll work it out. Stop worrying."

But he couldn't—because it was about him. But he wouldn't confess. Ever. He just couldn't.

Last night he'd dreamed he was in the middle of a game of dodge ball, but there was nowhere to dodge. He balanced on the top of the Fishers' gravel pile while Eric, Mom, Lily, V, and Frank threw basketballs at him. *Whap!* The ball hit his hand and his hand fell off. *Blap!* A direct hit to his leg, which broke off above the knee and tumbled, bloodless, down the mountain of gravel. *Boom!* Off went his head.

All his body parts kept growing back, faster and faster, only to be knocked off. Again and again.

Stop! Don't! he tried to shout in his sleep, but no real words came out, just crazy mangled sounds.

He remembered Lily waking him up, soothing him, saying everything was okay.

If only.

Next time she wanted to play cards, he would.

Lily

I knock on Eric's door.

"Abandon all hope, ye who enter here," he answers.

He is so weird.

"Lily!" he says, looking up from a skinny blue book. He's sitting on his bed, propped against a pillow with his knees bent up like mountain peaks.

He sounds surprised. That makes two of us, because I'm surprised to be here.

I glance around his room, amazed at how incredibly bare it is compared to mine and Parker's. We have stuff everywhere. Eric has nothing. A bookshelf full of old, beat-up books. A desk. One notebook computer with a skull drawing pasted on top. Tennis shoes that stink lying on the floor next to three socks. None of the socks match—unless you count the fact that all of them are dingy. Tan sheets on his bed—I guess Belks doesn't carry black ones. No bedspread. No posters.

It's as if he doesn't plan to stay more than one night.

"What's up?" he asks.

I panic. I haven't thought this out. What do I say first? *I have a plan to send soccer balls to Iraq? I have a plan to undo what I did to V's tomatoes? I have a plan because I've really missed having plans?*

"I need your help," I say.

"Me?" I swear, his eyes make a quick trip around the room to see if there's anyone else I could be talking to.

"You want me to rename your cat?" he asks.

"Huh?" Is he nuts? He's grinning though, so I guess it's some kind of a joke. For the first time, I notice some of V's movie-star good looks in Eric's face. He should smile more.

"Your cat. You know—Bubbles." He shrugs and slowly shakes his head. "Her name is as bad as Snowman's."

"What's the matter with 'Bubbles'?" I blurt out defensively, even though I know exactly what's wrong with it. It's a name I've wanted to take back a hundred times. I named her after a Powerpuff Girl a million years ago—when I was into all that.

He raises his eyes at me without lifting his head.

"Okay," I confess. "It's a dumb name. I know. And it doesn't fit. But what's so bad about 'Snowman'? He's white. He's male. He's round."

"It's a name only a little kid would dream up." Eric puts his book down on the bed, stretches his bony elbows up toward the ceiling, and yawns. "No imagination."

"But when you named him, you *were* a little kid," I argue.

He drops his arms and looks at me funny. I wonder if

he's wishing he was still a little kid. His dad expects a lot sometimes.

Whoa! I think, picturing him sprawled on the floor, playing with Parker, shooting baby laser guns at Darth Vader and the Incredible Hulk. Does he *want* to be younger?

Maybe. Maybe not.

Doesn't he read college-level books?

I still play with dolls sometimes, but that doesn't mean I wouldn't like to be the oldest again.

Weird—we both want to be the opposite thing.

Then I think about the fact that we both gave our pets stupid baby names, and that we both wish we could undo them.

What else did we have in common?

I think about the lame names some more.

"We can't rename them, you know. If we did that, they wouldn't be them."

"No," he says, sounding tired, then looking up at me with what I can only describe as respect. "They really wouldn't."

ERIC

Journal Entry #177

The old man is fighting the fish. Still. He is tired, surprisingly strong, and lonely.

Lily showed up in my room today. When was the last time she did that? When we moved in? When I told her what a metaphor was? No wonder she never came back.

Now, she needs help with a project—V was sending soccer balls to Iraq.

Who knew my sister could be so cool?

Actually, I knew, but not lately. Lately she's been toxic waste.

Lily wants to round up aluminum cans for the next four months—until I get my license. Then I drive them to the recycling center with her, and collect money.

I said sure, but I doubt she'll find enough cans to buy a Ping-Pong ball, much less a soccer one. She can't drive anywhere, and our neighborhood has about as much aluminum can litter as the front porch of the White House.

Is she doing it to make V happy? Or to make her feel guilty for not apologizing?

She seems too put-together for that.

Should I stay out of this? Or should I help her come up with a better idea?

Would that fulfill Dad's leadership requirement?

Parker

Eric came up with the best idea in the history of the world—a Rock-Paper-Scissors tournament. Parker couldn't wait.

One—it was going to be so much fun.

Two—it was going to make everybody forget about who killed Lily's flower.

Eric was in charge of buying prizes. Lily would head up advertising, because she's great with words, even if she thinks she's not. V was supposed to figure out all the math, like how much they could spend on prizes and still make enough money for soccer balls. Only, so far, she wasn't interested.

"You've got to be kidding," she'd said, then gone back to cracking eggs into a big mixing bowl. Yesterday she'd made the best blueberry cake Parker had ever tasted. Everybody, even Lily, said it could win the Pillsbury Bake-Off contest. No problem.

He couldn't wait to see what she was cooking next. Yummy cakes seemed a lot more useful than adding up a bunch of numbers for a tournament. But still, it made him sad she wasn't more excited about it. After all, the soccer balls had been her idea in the first place.

Parker was in charge of refreshments.

"You know," said Eric. "Make lemonade or something."

But Parker had a better idea. He'd been dying to try Papa Bud's suggestion. Cicadas. Low in calories. No carbs.

Eric has lost his mind. A Rock-Paper-Scissors tournament. To raise money for *my* soccer balls.

Who would enter? Eric has no friends. Lily has maybe two. Parker has plenty, but none of them have any money.

What a joke.

I didn't even care about the soccer balls anymore. And I didn't care that I was grounded. I had better things to do.

I made a blueberry cake yesterday and Mary Beth loved it. She asked what else I could cook.

"I have a terrific fudge recipe," I'd said. "Do we have any Baker's chocolate or Eagle Brand milk?"

Mary Beth opened the pantry cabinet and searched. She pulled out a dead-looking half of a chocolate bar. One whole corner was the color of chalk. "Just this," she said. "No Eagle Brand. I'll run to the store."

"I'll go with you," I said.

Here came that look again. Surprised. Puzzled. The one where she's discovering me for the very first time. How long would it take for her to get it?

In the car, I told her she should give me some chores to do at home. That I didn't mind. "I like vacuuming better than dusting. But I'm the best at organizing cabinets."

"V," she said, gripping the steering wheel as if it were a life preserver, "I appreciate the help. Really I do, but . . ."

She stopped at Sharon Road and looked both ways so many times I thought we'd take root.

"Mary Beth," I nudged her out of the coma she'd fallen into. "There's no traffic."

"Oh." She jumped, startled. She looked both ways again, then turned right.

"I don't know how to say this," she spoke softly.

"Say what?" Did she have some kind of disease where she had to do *everything* herself—no help allowed? Or did she think I would smash up her furniture with my lethal rake?

"Honey," she said.

"Yes," I answered. Please, whatever it is, just spit it out.

"You're not just trying to get yourself ungrounded, are you?"

If I'd been driving, I would've slammed on the brakes, gotten out of the car, and walked home.

"No," I snapped. "I'm not." What was wrong with this woman? All I wanted to do is what I'd always done—help Dad around the house. Hadn't I told her that? Should I tell her again?

"Mary Beth," I said, trying not to clench my teeth, "I know the only thing that will get me ungrounded is apologizing to Lily."

She turned toward me, her eyes warm and glistening. Oh,

no. Did she think that meant I *would* apologize to Lily? For something I didn't even do?

"I just like to make myself useful, okay?"

She nodded unconvincingly and pulled into the parking lot.

At Bi-Lo, I was so helpful I could've won a prize. I took half her grocery list, and met her with my part finished before she'd even pushed her cart midway down the produce aisle.

"V," she said, "I'm sorry about what I said in the car." She reached out, touched my arm, and smiled.

It was a start.

Lily

Eric trashed my aluminum can idea, and V is sucking up to Mom. I bet she thinks that if they become friends, she can get ungrounded without apologizing to me.

Ha! Mom would never fall for that.

Either way, I'm over it. I ripped up what was left of my sunflower. Frank said the busted stalk might recover and sprout another stem.

"Miracles," I told him, "don't happen anymore." I've learned about lots of them in Sunday school, but I can't name one thing that's happened lately. I figure Earth has rotated out of that cycle until further notice.

Besides, it makes me too sad to look at it.

My aluminum can–plan bit the dust, too, but that's okay. Because Eric's idea is even better. A Rock-Paper-Scissors tournament.

I'm in charge of advertising. All I need is a name. *The Hands Down Shakedown* or maybe *All Hands Get Decked*? What about *Hands Up! Your Money or Your Soccer Ball*?

The best part is that Parker and Eric and I are doing it together. If V wants to be a pain, that's her problem. I just wish I could figure some way to make it count as a science project.

Maybe I could get a stopwatch and time reflexes. Like whose hands move the fastest—male or female, young or old, fat or skinny? Or rich versus poor, smart against dumb, real against phony. What about people who destroy personal property and apologize for it, compared to people who don't?

According to Eric, Rock-Paper-Scissors *is* a science. There's actually a World RPS Society, founded in 1842, in London. They have strategies, rules, their own magazine, and a Player's Responsibility Code. No kidding. They even have personal trainers.

Eric already ordered an authentic RPS T-shirt as first prize for our grand champion. Winners of individual matches will get to take home an RPS sticker.

We haven't figured out the entry fee yet, because V won't do it. I'm useless with numbers and Parker's math hasn't gotten much past double digits yet. Eric could do it, but I think he's holding out, hoping V will join up.

He went ahead and ordered the prizes, though, because they take two weeks to get here, and we need to do this before school gets out if we expect anyone to show up.

There's a note on my door in Eric's handwriting.

RPS Meeting   NOW   My Room

When I walk in, Eric and Parker are already psyched.

"You wouldn't believe how many guys in my grade have already checked out the Web site. They're asking me questions like crazy. Major interest." He pulls me over. "Can you make up flyers for the school bulletin board?"

"Sure," I tell him. "I'll have them ready by tomorrow. Plus extra ones to nail on telephone poles in our neighborhood. How about the grocery store?"

"Yeah, sure," says Eric. "Why not?"

I give them my suggestions for names. Eric likes the *Hands Down Shakedown*. Parker wants *All Hands Get Decked*. I'm leaning towards *Hands Up! Your Money or Your Soccer Ball*.

We grin at each other and stick out our hands.

Pump, pump, pump.

My scissors immediately get smashed by two rocks.

Eric eyes his opponent, raises and lowers his eyebrows three times, and says to Parker, "I have mastered the Mystical School of RPS. My inner force is telling me what you're going to throw next."

"Wanna bet?" sneers Parker.

Pump, pump, pump.

Two rocks. No winner.

"What happened to your inner force?" jeers Parker.

"I'm just setting you up to fail," taunts Eric.

They raise their fists high into the air, then lower them slowly. They square off like two gunslingers at high noon.

Pump, pump, pump.

Eric's paper covers Parker's rock.

"I told you!" gloats Eric.

"Aw," groans Parker. "You got lucky."

"Not a chance," says Eric. "You blink twice every time you're about to throw a rock. You avalanched, man, and I saw it coming a mile away."

"Avalanched?" Parker and I ask at the same time.

"Three rocks in a row," explains Eric.

"Whoa!" I say. "Where'd you learn that?"

Eric taps his computer and grins. "There's a million of them."

"Cool," says Parker. "What else?"

"Gambits. That's what you call three throws in a row. They have names—like Avalanche. A Scissors Sandwich is paper-scissors-paper."

"Wait," I say. "I need to write this down. For my ads."

"Too much stuff," says Eric. "Just list the Web site."

"Good idea."

"Wait till I tell you what my refreshments are," says Parker. "They'll make more money than the tournament."

"Lemonade?" I ask.

"No!" he shouts. "Cicadas!"

"Sweet," says Eric.

"Chocolate covered, French fried, or hacked up into crunchy black sprinkles for ice cream." Parker's grin is stretched so tight across his new, permanent teeth, his lips could split.

Cicadas? Please tell me he's kidding.

Eric high-fives him. "Way to go, Mud Boy!"

Okay, I decide. Why not? He's got friends who would actually eat them.

Then an even better idea hits me.

"I know!" I exclaim. "We buy donuts—the ones with no holes—stick cicadas in them, and call them Insect-insides."

"Insecticides?" Eric tilts his head at me.

"Not insect-*i*-cide," I say. "Insect-*in*-side. Get it?"

Eric high-fives me.

Even Parker gets it. "Way to go, Lily," he says.

"Or we could stuff them in cupcakes," says Eric.

"Killer!" shouts Parker, jumping up and down. "Or cram them in Hostess Twinkies!"

"Perfect!" I exclaim. Then great idea number two hits me. "Hey! This *could* be a science project."

Eric is quiet for a second, thinking. Then he grins. "You could call it 'The Digestive Impact of Winged Insects on the Human Gastrointestinal Tract.'"

"Huh?" says Parker, who suddenly stops moving and stares.

"Nasty, scratchy, gassy guts," Eric explains, laughing out loud and punching the air.

"Cool!" exclaims Parker, happily hopping again. "Or 'Protein Twinkies'!" he shouts.

"'Protein Twinkies—Healthy or Hazardous?'" I scream.

We are all so pumped we may explode.

ERIC

Journal Entry #178

Gambits:

> *Avalanche = rock, rock, rock*
>
> *Bureaucrat = paper, paper, paper*
>
> *Toolbox = scissors, scissors, scissors*
>
> *Paper Dolls = p, s, s*
>
> *Fistful o' Dollars = r, p, p*
>
> *Crescendo = p, s, r*
>
> *Scissor Sandwich = p, s, p*

Rock—the most aggressive throw. Think of it as a weapon. Some players fall back on it when losing.

Scissors—the clever throw. Think of it as a tool. Arts and crafts. An outflanking maneuver used by confident players. Or, it can be considered aggressive. Think sharp—a weapon.

Paper—the most subtle. Some players think surrender—open palm. Others link paper to writing—power of the printed word. Know your opponent. Will he think paper is wimpy? Or strong?

Cloaking—*delay your throw intentionally. Trick a hand watcher into thinking you'll throw rock.*

Shadowing—*pretend to throw one thing, then switch at the last second. Caution: very risky—the ref may claim you changed too late. Safer to twitch fingers during the prime, then throw rock.*

Tells—*think poker player's face. Hand, face, or body movements broadcast opponent's next move. Personal trainer can help you watch.*

False tell—*let your opponent see your mannerisms, then fake him out.*

Important:

"Think twice before using RPS for life-threatening decisions."—*Rule #6 of The World RPS Player's Responsibility Code.*

Parker

Could the RPS tournament get any better?

Yes.

Frank was going to referee. Mom would charge a dollar to be anybody's personal trainer.

Thirty-two dollars in entry fees had been collected already, and word was spreading faster than the flu.

Parker wished V would help.

Lily

"This is going to be amazing," says Cassie, as she tapes another one of my RPS ads onto a gym locker.

"Yeah," I agree. I'm really proud of how well all this is working.

"And all of Eric's friends will be there!" she exclaims. "Who do you think is cuter, Will or Jason?"

Her question totally throws me. For two reasons.

One, I have never thought of tenth-grade boys as anything but scary.

And two, she's right. Eric has friends. Lots of them. They call our house ten times a day—asking Eric for RPS strategies. Asking where they can buy tickets. Asking if we're really going to eat bugs.

RPS has become the "in" thing for guys—grades nine through twelve. Girls are coming around slower, but there's hope. Yesterday, I swear I spotted Miss Prom Queen playing RPS with two friends behind the gym.

Parker has totally psyched grades K through four. I just pray we can get this tournament over with before the high school kids see all those hyper kindergartners and decide it's dumb.

I think we're safe. All the older kids are into meta-strategies like Rusty and Crystal Ball. And technical terms like "synching the prime," or knowing how many cubits of distance is legal between one fist and another.

"Well?" says Cassie.

"Well what?" I ask.

"Jason or Will?"

"Oh. I don't know. Jason, I guess."

Cassie sighs. "I like Will better."

Like it matters.

"Cassie," I feel forced to point out, "you do know that Jason and Will wouldn't notice us if we were"—I search frantically for a word—"naked."

Cassie giggles at the crazy picture that is suddenly in both of our heads. "Come on, Lily. They would, too."

She's right. They would. Suddenly I can't stop laughing, either.

Cassie tapes up two more ads, giggling softly to herself. Then she gets quiet and asks, "What about V? Is she helping with the tournament yet?"

"No," I say, "but she and Mom are BFF."

"No way!" says Cassie. "Your mom? And V? Best friends forever? How?"

"V volunteers for chores like it's some kind of Better Homes and Housekeeping contest."

"Doesn't that make you mad?"

"No." At least, I don't *think* it does. Mom needs help, and I'm way too busy with RPS and my science project to lose much sleep over V, even if she did kill my flower.

"I don't care what she does," I add in a voice that comes out way louder than I meant for it to.

"It'd make *me* mad." Cassie jams her hands on her hips. "I bet she's trying to get you back for hanging out with her dad in his workshop."

Sometimes Cassie is way too dramatic for me. "You should see how my science project is coming," I say. "I've researched everything there is to know about cicadas—where they live, whether you can eat them, what their nutritional value is. It's all drawn up on a poster, with pictures and everything. All I need to finish it are comments from the crazy people who eat them at the tournament."

"Do you really think anyone will do that?" Cassie makes a face like she swallowed a lemon.

"Parker's friends will. They can't wait." I tear off a strip of Scotch tape and hand it to her. "They'll scarf them down like Tic Tacs."

"Scarf? Does that mean eat?"

"Yeah."

"Did you know you talk funny since your family got teenagers?"

"Yeah."

"Cool." Cassie scans the locker room, then tapes one more ad over the exit door. "Your bug project's cool, too," she says. "Mrs. Finley will wear out her red marker writing, 'Inventive! Ingenious! Imaginative!'"

I twist my mouth into an even barfier version of Cassie's previous yuck face and add, "'Indigestion.'"

I lean over, pick up my leftover ads, and slide them neatly inside my backpack.

It makes me feel good that Cassie thinks I talk older. But what about the other thing she said? About V and Mom? *Is* V getting me back?

"So," I ask Cassie, "do you really think Mrs. Finley will like it?"

"Totally," she says.

"I hope so." I zip my pack closed with one firm, fast motion. "That'll show V she's not the only one who can make an A."

Cassie turns and gives me a confused look.

"What?" I ask.

"Nothing," she says. "Only . . ." She hesitates. "Two minutes ago, you said you didn't care what V does."

Hi! This is Misty, breathed a soft voice. *I'm out right now, but leave your number and I'll ring back.*

"Misty?" I stared at the telephone. Since when had Melissa, *my* mother, become *Misty*? And *ring back*? Who said that? Not my mom.

Had living in L.A. made her go Hollywood? Was she trying to land some movie part where she needed to sound sexy and stupid?

Why not? I never heard from her anymore, so anything was possible.

I missed my mom.

I missed Ben.

I missed Chicago.

Heck, I even missed Eric—the brother who's here, but not here. And sharing Dad was taking some getting used to. But at least Mary Beth had discovered me. Finally.

She promised to take me to the new Italian market today— the one that just opened next to the Better Bread Basket. Would all these new specialty shops hurt Dad's fresh-foods grocery business? I felt a little bit like a traitor shopping at

Milvio's, but they carry real Tuscan spices for my spaghetti, and Dad's stores don't.

I wandered off looking for him, thinking, he's gotten extra good olive oil shipped in from Italy before. Why not spices?

I stopped.

The door to his workshop gaped wide open. "I'm proud of you," came Dad's voice from inside.

My ears burned. Was he talking to Lily? Proud of *her* for *my* soccer-ball idea?

"No big deal," muttered Eric.

Eric! Dad was talking to Eric.

Proud of him for what? My soccer-ball idea?

I wouldn't mind that.

"It is a big deal," answered Dad. "You've earned enough money to buy your own car—"

"Hearse," said Eric.

I could hear Dad sigh all the way from where I was eavesdropping.

"I'd rather you bought a car," he said. "But it's your money, son. And you've done your homework on the insurance. And even raised enough money for that, too. I'm extremely proud of you."

Silence.

Dad's voice was warm and fuzzy. Practically glowing. Exactly what Eric needed. Why didn't he answer? Can he hear only negative-Dad?

"How's the RPS plan coming?" asked Dad.

"Fine," said Eric, in a way that really meant, *can I go now?*

Fine? How uninformative could you get?! Where was the Eric who exploded with RPS ideas? The Eric who wanted me to figure out the profits for the best moneymaking project in the history of the world?

"Is V helping?" Dad asked.

"No." Eric's voice shot out through the open door, hard and flat.

"Son," said Dad in a sympathetic tone, "all this has been hard on V."

"All what?" answered Eric, his voice rising.

"Our new family . . . her mom—gone . . . Ben." The last word a whisper. "It's difficult for her."

"Her?!" Eric exploded. *"Her?!"*

"It's difficult for you, too," said Dad. "But you're older. And easier, and—"

Easier? What did Dad mean, Eric was easier? Didn't I help around the house, and get good grades, and . . . and . . . communicate! For God's sake, *I'm* easy!

"I'll do what I can," muttered Eric.

The scraping sound of my chair meant Eric was getting up. I rushed back into the house and slammed the door, ready to bolt straight into the seclusion of my room.

"How's my Italian spice girl?" exclaimed Mary Beth, standing by the kitchen door dangling her car keys in one hand, her hair up in a twist. "Ready to go?"

"Um . . . what . . . no," I said, panicking. Fighting back tears.

The last thing I wanted to do was be in a car with Mary Beth. With anybody!

Which was worse? For her to see me crying? Or to seem difficult for not going?

I swallowed the ache in my throat and swiped at my eyes.

"Sure—let's go. I'm easy," I lied.

ERIC

Journal Entry #179

Dad expects me to be Superman. Like I can fix everything—and everybody.

He hates my hearse.

Journal Entry #180

"Eat my shorts."—*Bart Simpson*

Lily

I thought tournament day would never get here, but it has. Tomorrow a jillion people will magically appear in our backyard, ready to do hand-battle and spend money. I hope.

The RPS stickers and the grand prize T-shirt finally got here. A very cutting-it-close two days ago. Eric has been losing it all week. Not the package. His cool.

"The tracking number says it's in Atlanta!" he screamed. "Yesterday it was in New York! It flew *over* us!"

"Maybe Atlanta is a sorting hub," said Mom. "You know, a checkpoint location where everything has to go before it comes here."

"And maybe it's not," Eric groaned.

Even Frank looked worried. But he was clearly trying to stay out of our plans. He's big on all of us being leaders. Especially Eric.

But, the prizes did finally get here. The stickers are funky, and the T-shirt is worth every penny of its $18.50 price tag. It's black with a medium-sized blue circle. Inside the circle are three muscle-men silhouettes throwing rock, paper, and scissors. Every player will want it so bad they'll enter twice—maybe three times.

Eric would kill for it—it's so *him*.

Everything else is almost ready. Parker and I are in the kitchen, stuffing scaly frozen cicadas into Hostess Twinkies. We totally messed up the first three, until we figured out that we needed to fold the wings tighter and stuff them in headfirst.

I especially try not to look at their beady red eyes and wonder how they'd taste. Or even worse—*feel*. Do insect eyes crunch or squish?

The only good thing about this project is that when I cram a cicada in, half the filling squirts out. Which means I get to eat the creamy part.

Parker went nuts when he got to the grocery store with Mom. He discovered Shrek Twinkies, specially made with ogre-green cream filling instead of the regular white stuff. "Same great taste!" shouted the box.

So he freaked and bought twelve 10-packs. Even I can figure out that that's 120 non-returnable gross-colored Twinkies!

Mom tried to talk him out of it, but somehow he convinced her that he'd make a profit. He's planning to sell them for double the forty-two dollars of our ticket money that he paid for them. But 120! I think that's way too many. He thinks it's way not enough.

I try to do more math.

We've sold fifty-four tickets so far, which gives us $108, minus $42 for Twinkies, $9.60 for lemonade, and $33.50 for prizes. Plus $25 that Papa Bud donated, minus $6 a ball for postage, minus another $1.75 for the three Twinkies we ruined and the two that Parker ate. All of which means we can buy . . . I don't know how many balls.

V says, with the 50 percent discount she talked the Sport Shop into, we can buy three good ones or six crummy ones. Maybe even a few more if we find a cheaper way to ship them, but a whopping five to nine more if Parker sells out of his bug snacks. The Insectinsides are clearly our biggest profit item. *If* they're a hit.

And one monster-green loss if they're not.

The whole thing reminds me of impossible word problems. Like if Jack has ten dollars to buy twenty apples that are scheduled to arrive Tuesday on a river barge traveling upstream at thirty miles an hour, will the apples be red or green?

Thank goodness, V has decided to help. Numbers make my brain ache.

Lately, she's been strange, though. Agreeing out of nowhere to keep the money totals for the tournament. One day she just appeared, smiled as if everything in our stressed-out house was normal, and said, "I'm in."

Too bad she didn't take over the books before Parker overspent half our money.

Since then, she's painted my toenails Cranberry Crazy, told me I had pretty teeth, cut my hair so it actually has style, and talked me into getting two new tops that aren't T-shirts. She even gave me two good suggestions for improving my science project. Still no apology, but she's clearly going for a gold medal in getting along.

Fine. Papa Bud always says it's important to turn the other cheek. So I'm trying to get over it. Move on. Forgive and forget.

Besides, Eric told me that hanging on to old hurts won't make anybody miserable but me. Did he read that in one of his books, or did he learn it the hard way?

Whichever. Today, I'm more worried about how many people will eat Parker's cicadas. Cassie thinks more people will show up than the ones who actually compete. I hope so.

I also hope they like Insect-insides. A lot. But just in case they don't, I'm going to put out a donation jar. I called the newspaper to place an ad, but it was way too expensive. So totally beyond our budget that I didn't have to do any math to figure it out—no way, José.

"Stop eating the Twinkies!" I yell at Parker, who apparently thought I wasn't looking.

"Look!" screeches V, rushing into the room clutching

a newspaper. Her face is radiating so much panic I wonder if she's just read about a permanent ban on nail polish.

"What?" I ask, licking cream off my finger, and getting a yummy whiff of sugar and moist yellow sponge cake in spite of the slime green color. Fortunately, frozen cicadas have almost no smell at all.

"This!" she shouts, thrusting the paper in my face.

"Election Primaries Postponed," I read.

"No!" she says. "The headline under that."

"Cicada Allergy Kills Forty-Three-Year-Old Man"

"Kills!" I exclaim. "Kills how?"

"He ate one," says V, waving her hands. "And he died."

Parker's eyes open rounder than the plates we're stacking the Twinkies on. His mouth falls open.

"Did he choke?" Parker asks feebly.

"No," says V. "He had an allergy to shellfish. And maybe that made him have an allergic reaction to bugs. And maybe it didn't. The doctors don't know."

Parker blinks a couple of times, clearly trying to focus on what this means. Then he closes his mouth, stands as tall as he can, and announces, "Okay. So. We won't sell any cicadas to allergic people."

I feel so sad. For him. For me. For all of us. We can never sell the cicadas now, and I know it.

"Fine by me," says V, faking a half-hearted smile. "I'm easy."

What is with her? All of a sudden, "I'm easy" has become her favorite expression. Of course we can't feed people killer cicadas! Is she crazy?

I stare at our piles of Insect-insides. A hundred and twenty little bitty possible death traps—minus five.

A third of our profits. Gone. Or would it be more like half? Two-fifths?

I have no clue what percentage of our money just dropped directly into the garbage can. But I do know that *all* of my science project just got an F.

Parker

"Nobody's gonna die!" Parker screamed at everyone in Eric's room.

V, Eric, and Lily stared at him while he waved his hands in the air and stomped his bare foot.

"Hey, Mud Boy. Relax," said Eric in a super-calm voice. "It'll be okay."

"No, it won't!" Parker shouted. He balled his fists up so tight that his knuckles hurt.

"We've still got your lemonade to sell," said Lily quietly. "We just won't make quite as much money."

Parker wanted to hit her. She's the one who'd thought all along that he'd spent too much money. Well, actually everyone had thought that, but Lily was the one who'd said, "Parker, you are so stupid."

V didn't say anything.

"It definitely sucks, though," Eric admitted.

"Yeah," echoed Parker. "Sucks."

"But we've got no choice," said Eric.

"Noooooo," Parker moaned, stomping his foot again.

"We can't chance it," said Eric. "How would you feel if

someone ate one of your cicadas, then fell over dead?"

Parker rolled his eyes. "Nobody's going to do that."

"They might," said Eric.

"Besides," added Lily. "Mom and Frank agree. No cicadas."

"Talk to them," Parker begged, looking straight at V. Wasn't she on his side? "Talk to your dad. Pleeeeze."

"Ha!" squeaked V. "Don't look at me. Try Eric."

"Me?" Eric asked, dumbfounded.

"You're the one he's so proud of," muttered V, looking down.

"Dad?" said Eric in amazement. "Have you lost your mind? Dad thinks I'm a total loser."

"He said he's proud of you. I heard him."

"When?"

"I don't know. A couple of weeks ago. In his workshop. He said he was proud that you earned the money for—"

"Oh. That," said Eric. "He didn't mean that. He meant—"

"Eric," V interrupted. "He expects a lot. But not half as much as you think. You don't listen."

"What about our cicadas?" shouted Parker.

Eric stared blankly into space for a second, then jerked his head slightly as if he were shaking out something that didn't belong there.

"Don't worry," he answered, moving his full attention back to Parker. "We'll make up the loss in entry fees. Go get on the phone. Now. Make all of your friends call everyone they know. Lily and V, you, too. And more signs—especially on the main roads into the neighborhood."

Would that help? Parker wondered. Maybe. If Eric said so.

"RPS! RPS!" roared Eric, pumping his fist over and over and throwing an Avalanche.

"RPS!" yelled Lily and V, both of them spreading their fists flat—into paper.

"Scissors," shouted Parker, lunging at Lily with his first two fingers opened wide.

Then he shot out of Eric's room and down the hall to the phone. Who should he call first? Jay? Edward? Anna?

He picked up the receiver and punched in the numbers to Edward's house.

"Hello?" Edward answered.

"It's me. Mud Boy," said Parker, excited.

"Bug Man!" Edward shouted back. "Tomorrow! I can't wait! I'm going to eat at least one. Definitely. Maybe two. But I've dared George that he can't eat three. And I'm practicing my throws. Right now. I bet I win. Should I eat bugs before or after the contest? What if I throw up? Maybe I better eat after—"

"Uh . . . Mom's calling me," Parker muttered. "Gotta go." He clicked off the phone.

All his friends were expecting insect food. They would

kill him. Or call him a wuss. It wasn't fair. What had he done wrong? Nothing.

Then he remembered. Lily's flower. Was this somehow connected to that? Was he being punished? He tried to remember what he'd learned in Sunday school. Did this have anything to do with the God who sent a flood to wash away all those people who messed up? What about the God who said everybody should forgive everybody their trespasses?

And what the heck was a trespass, anyway?

Parker never could keep that stuff straight. It was too confusing.

He hoped none of his friends showed up.

ERIC

Journal Entry #181

I hope all my friends show up. And all their friends. We're going to need a chunk of money to cover the cicada loss.

So freaky. I mean, some old dude actually <u>died</u>!

Mud Boy—poor kid. It's not his fault, even if he did spend too much money.

I wish I had more time to write—RPS keeps me too busy.

<u>Good</u> writing I mean. Like the train metaphor.

I finished The Old Man and the Sea *a long time ago, but it hangs with me—awesome.*

As a writer, Hemingway is dead-on. When he writes clean and simple, it sounds like a poem. When I write that way, it sounds like a list.

Journal Entry #182

"I like to listen. I have learned a great deal from listening carefully. Most people never listen." —*Ernest Hemingway*

V's crazy.

I listen.

Definitely.

Carefully?

Maybe.

Maybe not.

Lily

I hope I never see another Twinkie as long as I live.

My stomach feels like it's full of a billion worms, all trying to wiggle their way out of wet, green cement. How much ogre-cream filling did I eat?

I want to die.

No.

I just want to throw up.

Please, God, let me barf.

Now!

I swatted at a yellow jacket buzzing around one of our lemonade cups, then wished I hadn't wasted the motion. It was so hot I had little beads of sweat trickling down the back of my neck, and it wasn't even June yet. I swear, it was stickier and hotter than when we moved here last August.

"Is it always this hot in May?" I asked Parker.

"Hot?" He stared at me like *huh?*

Don't little kids notice heat?

Luckily, a lot of other people didn't seem to notice, either, because our backyard filled up with people—all sizes, shapes, and ages. A mom with two babies asleep in a double stroller leaned against the side of Dad's workshop, chatting away with Mrs. Schwartz, who lived three houses down. One wiry-haired, short kid and his lots-taller buddy glided down our driveway on scooters. A skinny elf-girl showed up straight from gymnastics class still wearing her leotard. And a bent-over old guy gripped a cane with one hand while he searched his pocket for lemonade money with the other. One shiny black car full of jocks screeched up to the curb with the car speakers booming.

Bubbles blasted herself into hiding so fast she could've been a missile. Snowman bounced around, licking the ankles of every-one in sight. Parker and I manned the lemonade stand.

Poor kid.

Mary Beth had had to drag him out of bed.

"Don't make me go," he'd begged.

"Don't be silly," she'd laughed.

But it wasn't funny. His friends were going to be bummed out big time when they discovered there were no cicada-Twinkies to munch on—except for a few lying dead under an azalea bush somewhere.

But Eric swooped to the rescue. While Lily and I were say-ing lame things to Parker like "Your friends will get over it" and "You don't want someone to die, do you?" Eric showed up with a box of small plastic bags and a bowl full of Twinkie chunks he'd fished out of the garbage.

"Death Crumbs!" he announced victoriously.

"Huh?" said Parker, venturing his head out from under his sheet like a wary turtle.

Eric handed Parker a permanent black laundry marker and a bag, and ordered, "Here you go, Mud Boy. Write 'Death Crumbs—Do Not Eat' on each bag. Then I'll fill them with a little used Twinkie litter."

Everyone stared at him.

"This was all I could save." Eric gazed apologetically at the small bowl in his hand, which had only a few smashed yellow cake pieces in the bottom. "Dad dumped coffee grounds into the garbage can, right on top of the trashed Twinkies," he explained.

A spark of life flickered faintly in Parker's eyes.

"But Mom said we can't sell Twinkie scraps," he said in a quiet, un-Parker-like voice. "Because of the restidoo."

"Residue," I whispered.

I'm trying not to correct people, but sometimes it slips out.

Mary Beth had said that, even if Parker took the cicadas out of the Twinkies, they could still be contaminated—with residue.

Right. Like a piece of leftover insect knee could actually kill somebody!

"Don't tell her," said Eric.

"Don't tell her?" Parker echoed in amazement, as if he'd never done a single sneaky thing in his entire angel life.

"Well," said Eric. "You can tell her—if she asks. But if she doesn't ask . . ." He cut his eyes sideways and shrugged. "Look," he added, as if he needed to sound more responsible, "she said don't sell any for food. This," he declared, holding up a bag, "will clearly say, 'Do Not Eat.'"

So Parker and I ended up selling lemonade in the backyard, looking like two nice, all-American kids, but we had Death Crumbs stashed under the tablecloth like so many bags of illegal drugs.

A bunch of guys my age hung around, not buying anything, but Parker's friends came ready to blow their allowances big time. Too bad there weren't enough life-threatening bags to make much money, but at least Parker saved face.

"Whoa," said all his friends. "Death Crumbs . . . Killer!"

Then they hid them in their pockets to be pulled out later, and admired forever, or until ants someday found holes in the plastic.

The only non-kid we sold a bag to was Papa Bud, who winked and promised not to tell. He's one okay guy after all. He even donated $25 to the soccer cause.

I'd forgotten what it was like to feel this good.

Lily

I feel more like me than I have since Mom got married.

The RPS tournament is going great, in spite of the fact that it's super hot and humid. Even better, everyone in my family is helping. And I am the one who brought the whole idea back from the dead.

One project saved.

One to go.

I have no clue what I'm going to do for science now.

How about, "Cream Filling: The Sickening Effects of Excessive Consumption"?

If only I'd thrown up on a poster board last night, instead of in the toilet, I could've labeled the poster "Exhibit A" and turned it in to Mrs. Finley with an essay on "Why Isn't Your Stomach Connected to Your Brain?"

But the best news is that a reporter from the *Charlotte Observer* is here to write a newspaper article on the *Hands Down Shakedown*.

We'll all be famous.

"Whose idea was it for the tournament?" asks this tall

guy who doesn't look much older than Eric. He pulls out a tiny tape recorder and turns it on.

"It was my brother Eric's idea," I tell him, and wonder if he'll play my voice back to me later. I think it's amazing how my own voice on tape always sounds like someone I've never even met.

"But my sister, V, came up with the soccer-ball plan," I continue. "And my little brother, Parker—call him Mud Boy—wanted to sell cicadas to eat, which I named Insect-insides, but Mom won't let him because they might kill somebody."

Am I talking too fast? Do I sound too young? I try to dredge up some of my new mature vocabulary that Cassie noticed, but I'm too excited.

And why did I tell the reporter to call my brother Mud Boy, when I don't even like that name? I don't know. I guess because I know how excited Parker will be to see it in print.

The reporter wipes a trickle of sweat off his forehead, asks more questions, and keeps taping. Then he wanders off to interview more people and watch the matches.

They go great. Some people even enter more than once, so maybe we're making money. Who knows?

The grand prize T-shirt is hanging from a tree over the table where Eric is selling tickets. I watch him grin with pride every time somebody comments on how great it is. I know how much he wants to own it.

Which is why I'm stunned when he says he isn't going to compete for it. As a matter of amazing fact, he says that no one in our family should enter.

"What?" we all scream.

"It'd be like Bob Barker winning *The Price is Right*," he says.

Who?

"Or Alex Trebek walking off with all the *Jeopardy!* cash. You can't go around winning your own game." Eric crosses his long arms over his chest and adds, "Bad policy."

It's okay, though. All of us are too busy running the tournament to compete anyway.

"And the winner of heat number twenty-two is Javonne Townsend!" shouts Frank, holding up the hand of a ninth grader as if she were the champion of a boxing match. Eric hands her a sticker with a fist against a red background, and Javonne walks off grinning like she'd won the biggest lottery in the history of the world.

Personal trainer Mom is busy instructing her next client, a small freckle-faced boy named C. J.

"Don't let his size and age scare you," she says, pointing to his high school opponent—a huge football guy with muscles like rocks. "You'll smear him."

C. J. steps cautiously up onto the small square stage

that Frank built about a foot off the ground. He sticks his fist out approximately one cubit from his opponent's monster knuckles, and scrunches up his face as if he's about to cry.

"Ready?" says football guy.

"Ready," squeaks C. J.

Pump, pump, splat.

With his last hand motion, C. J. has slapped a mosquito on his forearm.

"Foul," says Frank gently.

C. J.'s lower lip starts to tremble.

"Objection!" shouts Mom. "Lily! Go get the citronella candles out of the cabinet in the garage. We've got to get rid of these mosquitoes. Okay," she states, "start over. C. J. gets another chance."

I hear the football guy protest, "But Mrs. Evans, you're not the referee."

"Fraaank," Mom drawls in a sweet voice that really means agree with me, honey. Now.

When I return with the candles, the rematch is over and C. J. has won. He is so cute—I hope he wins the whole thing.

Football guy is getting in line to buy another ticket. And Mom is standing under a dogwood tree, pushing her hair back and explaining gambit play to her next client, a white-haired old man who walks with a cane.

I light the Bug-Away candles and the weird, sweet smell of citronella soaks the air. Between that and the lemonade, our yard smells like a fruit fest.

V is a boy-magnet at the refreshment stand. Even the reporter person is flirting with her. I hope they're all spending money.

Cassie hangs around the boy-swarm for a while, then gives up and plays RPS. She wins her heat! I am so excited for her! What if the final match comes down to Cassie and C. J.? Who will I pull for?

But it doesn't. Mrs. DeVaughan—the lady V babysits for and whose son is stationed in Iraq—ends up in the final pairing. She stands on the wooden stage in her trendy red sandals, ironed sleeveless T-shirt, and cropped flowered pants. Opposite her is football guy, because he won the rest of his heats after he bought a second ticket.

The prize goes to the first person to win three throws.

Frank bends over and squints at the distance between their hands. He nods and says, "May the best gambit win."

"Ready?" says muscle guy, leaning in and flexing his biceps.

"Ready," says Mrs. DeVaughan, narrowing her eyes like a snake.

Pump, pump, pump.

Paper covers rock. Mrs. DeVaughan wins the first throw. Yes!

But I see her move her fingers just before the throw, telegraphing the fact that she's going to do something other than rock. Did football guy see it?

"Ready?"

"Ready."

Pump, pump, pump.

She wiggles her fingers again! But this time she throws scissors. Football guy throws scissors. A tie. I had him figured for a three-rock gambit—an Avalanche—but he must have thought she would throw paper twice.

The crowd is going wild. Shouts of *Go Ellen! Go Mrs. DeVaughan! Go Malcolm!* split the air.

Football guy is Malcolm?

Pump, pump, pump.

Mrs. DeVaughan does the telling finger wiggle again and throws scissors. Malcolm throws paper. What was he thinking?

He slaps his forehead, knowing he messed up. Perspiration explodes off his face, spraying Frank and Mrs. DeVaughan.

"Sorry," Malcolm apologizes.

"That's perfectly all right," answers Mrs. DeVaughan courteously. She's not even breaking a sweat.

"No problem," mutters Frank, wiping his cheek.

Mrs. D has won two throws and tied one. One more win and the RPS championship is hers!

I want to scream at her, "Don't throw rock!" Because if football guy doesn't see any finger movement, he'll know a rock is coming. But with her wiggle giveaway on the others, he'll have to guess—paper or scissors?

"Ready?"

"Ready."

"Go Ellen! Go Malcolm!"

Everyone is cheering. Snowman is jumping up onto my shins with excitement.

Pump, pump, pump.

Mrs. DeVaughan doesn't move her fingers! She's going to throw a rock! I know it. Malcolm knows it.

He throws paper.

Mrs. D throws scissors!

She wins!

The crowd roars! Snowman is cutting frenzied figure eights in and out of a million legs.

Mrs. DeVaughan tricked him with a false tell! So brilliant!

Eric sprints over with the RPS T-shirt and jerks it over her head.

Mrs. DeVaughan throws her hands up in the air and screams something that sounds like "Whaaaaeeeeee!"

She looks like a crazed little kid in a too-big shirt.

The crowd leaves pretty fast after that. I pour two cups of lemonade down my sore-from-screaming throat, and dash off to get Snowman a big dish of water. That's when I remember that I forgot to put out a donation jar.

Mrs. DeVaughan tells Eric that she'll probably give the shirt to her son in Iraq since it will fit him better. "I can't wait to tell him all about this," she says excitedly. "You kids are incredible! When will you know how many soccer balls you'll be able to send?" she asks. She's as eager to know as we are.

"As soon as we figure up our profits," Eric answers.

We all look over at V, who is busy adding up the money in the cash box and writing numbers down on a yellow legal pad.

She is not smiling.

HANDS DOWN SHAKEDOWN

BY RANDALL MERCER

Staff Writer

What does it mean when a hundred people show up in a quiet Charlotte neighborhood shaking their fists? A Rock, Paper, Scissors tournament, that's what. This project, the brainchild of V Stone, was created to raise money to send soccer balls to children in Iraq, and was carried out with the help of her sister and brothers.

Dozens of people of all ages competed in the timeless children's game in which the shape of a hand determines the winner. Rock smashes scissors. Scissors cut paper. Paper covers rock. The grand-prize winner, Ellen DeVaughan (whose son Daniel is stationed in Iraq) received a much-coveted T-shirt, from the World RPS Society, which was founded in London in 1842.

The event was a giant success in terms of fun, but less triumphant as a fund-raiser. V Stone's Insect-insides (her clever name for Twinkies stuffed with cicadas) had to be withdrawn from the refreshment stand due to health risks, resulting in a substantial loss of profits. The Stone children still plan to send at least four soccer balls to Iraq.

Regardless of the outcome, the initiative and generosity of these young people is to be applauded.

Lily

V Stone's Insect-insides!
Her clever name!
The Stone children!
I can't believe V grabbed all the credit!
Just when I thought she was turning human.
I don't even have a name.

My Insect-insides!
My clever name!
The Stone children!

Who is Randall Mercer and why hasn't he been fired? Where did he get his facts?

Lily and Parker's last name is Evans, not Stone. And they do have *first* names for God's sake! The name "Insect-insides" was Lily's idea. RPS was Eric's!

I didn't tell him any of that other stuff!

But who's going to believe me?

And why does this keep happening to me?

Parker

"Reporters get facts confused all the time," said Mom, trying to patch up the huge hole that had just blown wide open again in the middle of the family.

Lily glared at V.

V stuck her chin up in the air as if to say, *I don't care anymore*.

Eric sat slouched in a chair, one leg thrown over the arm, reading a book.

"Remember when Frank's first store opened?" Mom continued, almost pleading. "And the newspaper gave the wrong address?"

Nobody remembered. At least nobody said they did.

Parker couldn't believe this was happening. Just when everything had been looking good again. He hadn't even had a nightmare where his head got knocked off in over a week.

Plus, Eric had said you don't have to confess things if nobody asks. Hadn't he said that?

So now what was he supposed to do? Lily hated V again, and V was acting all stuck-up and claiming that she never told the dumb reporter any of those things. He just got his facts mixed up.

But nobody believed V, because V was a proven liar.

Except Parker knew she wasn't.

And why, he groaned to himself, had Mom let him buy too many stupid Twinkies?

ERIC

Journal Entry #183

We read A Tale of Two Cities *in English class. Now we're ending the year with poetry. A poet named W. H. Auden wrote,*

"The kitchen table exists because I scrub it."

Which made me think that my kitchen table exists because Dad built it, and how much roomier it is than the old one, but that—am I crazy?—I miss the crowded one.

Mostly we're reading sonnets about love and flowers. I'd rather read Hemingway.

Lily

Thank you, Cassie.

For being my friend.

"Look," she says, sprawled out on my bed while I slump over my desk, cleaning pencil stubs and old papers out of my drawer. "Forget about V. I mean, you just have to live with her for a few more years, not marry her."

She has a point. I think.

I examine an empty CD case, wondering where the disk went. "But I wanted a fun sister. One who doesn't lie," I add.

"Doesn't everybody?" Cassie replies.

Another good point.

"Besides," she says, "you don't need any kind of sister right now. You need a science project."

Oh, yeah. Do I ever.

I wad up the *Hands Down Shakedown* newspaper article, which has somehow ended up on my desk, and pitch it at the wastebasket. I've pretty much decided to turn in my cicada research without the final results and hope I get a passing grade. Unless my lost fairy godmother suddenly remembers she's got a daughter in Charlotte that she forgot.

Cassie scoops up the ball of newspaper that missed the wastebasket and flattens it back out. As I watch her read V's lies, I notice the headline on the back: *Birth Order Affects Personality*.

Huh?

Suddenly V flies into my room shouting, "Lily! You've got to see this! Where's Parker? Hi, Cassie. Where's Eric? Look!"

Cassie and I stare at V, who is holding a stack of opened envelopes. She pulls a check out of one and hands it to me.

I stare at a blue personal check for $10 made out to V Stone and signed by somebody named Martin Witherspoon. Who is Martin Witherspoon?

She hands me a pale green one signed by Mary Rodriquez.

"Donations!" shrieks V, then shoots out of the room shouting, "Parker! Eric!"

A few seconds later, they're all back in my room, and we're counting money. People who saw the newspaper article have sent money!

We cheer and jump up and down and whoop. Mom comes in, then Frank, and we all cheer some more, then rush out of the house, straight to Swenson's for ice cream sundaes to celebrate. Cassie comes, too.

The minivan seats only six, so we get ready to pile into two cars.

Eric says, "If I had a hearse, we could all ride together."

"What about seat bel—" Frank starts to say, but shuts up when Mom elbows him in the ribs. "Yeah, son. We sure could."

At Swenson's we all order different flavors of ice cream and sit in a huge booth.

"How much money?" Parker asks V. He's jiggling up and down as if he's riding an invisible pony.

"Fifty-seven dollars," she answers. "But the newspaper said they wouldn't be surprised if they forward us even more envelopes over the next few weeks."

"This is so unbelievable," says Mom, spooning up a bite of French vanilla with caramel sauce.

"Who would have thought?" says Cassie, licking butter pecan off a cone.

"Did you know that babies are born without kneecaps?" says Frank.

We all look at him as if he has lost his mind.

"Dad," says V, "what has that got to do with—"

"Unbelievable things," says Frank, with a mouthful of chocolate macadamia nut crunch. "We were talking about unbelievable things, right?"

"Peanuts are one of the ingredients in dynamite," says Eric.

"Really?" says Mom, amazed.

"It's impossible to sneeze with your eyes open," says Cassie.

Parker tries to fake a sneeze, but instead sprays the whole table with half-chewed chunks of banana split and fudge sauce.

"Parker!" shouts Mom, giving him an irritated look.

"Sorry," says Parker. "I was just—"

"There's nothing in the English language that rhymes with purple," I say, hoping to distract Mom from Parker's mess.

"Burple does," declares Parker, vigorously wiping the table with his napkin.

"Burple?" Frank asks, lowering his chin and raising his eyebrows into a "what the heck is burple?" face.

"Yeah," says Parker. Then he lets out a belch that turns every head in the place. *Burp-ull!*

Only Eric laughs.

"Gross," says V.

I agree.

Frank glares his disapproval while Mom makes a shush sign at Parker with her fingers.

Parker slumps into a pout.

"A dime has one hundred and eighteen ridges around the edge," says V.

"And a quarter has two million!" screams Parker.

"You can't just make things up," I tell him.

"I didn't!" he yells back.

"Did you know that 'dreamt' is the only word in English that ends in the letters mt? says Mom.

"You made that up," objects Parker, banging his ice cream spoon on the table. "'Dreamt' is not a word."

"Shhh," cautions Mom. "Keep it down."

"Actually," says Eric, "'dreamt' is a word. Poets use it." Parker droops into another pout.

"Come on, buddy," says Frank encouragingly. "I bet you can think of something true that no one else knows. Did you know that butterflies have twelve thousand eyes?"

Parker squirms and pulls on his shirt, as if cicadas were crawling on him. He's not even listening.

"Did you know that nothing rhymes with 'orange'?" I say.

"Or 'silver,'" adds V.

"Or 'whistle,'" Parker adds stubbornly.

"How about 'thistle'?" says V, and then I can tell she wishes she'd just agreed with him. Suddenly, we all do. Because Parker is about to blow. Explode. Bust wide open if he can't think of something nobody else knows.

"Did you know that I killed Lily's flower?" he shouts.

"Did you know that I killed Lily's flower?" Parker shouted.

For a second, I thought he was making it up, just like he had when he'd blurted out that a quarter had two million ridges.

But then I looked at his face.

His eyes widened in surprise, as if he couldn't believe what had just leaped out of his mouth. Then they filled up with tears and spilled over onto his cheeks.

"It was an accident," he whispered. "I didn't mean to."

"You what?" said Dad, lowering his spoon and staring at Parker.

"My sunflower," said Lily, looking totally bewildered. "You?"

Mary Beth and Eric gaped at Parker with their mouths slightly open. Speechless.

"Lily," whimpered Parker. "I'm really sorry."

Lily! I thought. What about me? I've been taking the blame for your crime for weeks!

"V," he hiccupped, looking up at me and wiping tears away with the palms of both hands. Watered-down fudge sauce smeared across his cheeks. He hiccupped a couple more times before he finally managed to squeak out, "I'm sorry I . . . I . . . let them blame you."

I tried to squeeze out a forgiving grin, but it got stuck halfway and probably ended up looking pretty pinched. "It's okay," I told him. "I'm easy."

Dad's eyebrows raised in surprise. He reached across the table, squeezed my hand, and gave me a small, proud smile. Then he turned to Parker.

"Now, young man, what do you have to say for yourself?"

Which was such a typical stupid-parent thing to say, because he'd already told us exactly what he had to say for himself—he was sorry. And he was crying. And he was clearly pitiful. Come on, Dad. Take a look.

Parker didn't answer. Instead he lowered his head and said, "Everybody hates me." Then he glanced up at Eric.

"Man, Mud Boy," said Eric. "You are in deep doo-doo."

Which—hooray for Eric—made everybody laugh out loud.

Even Dad chuckled. He didn't even cut Eric one of his looks that said, *please grow up and give the kindergarten bathroom words a break.*

I hoped Eric was listening—to the part Dad hadn't said.

"You're not mad?" Parker nervously asked the whole table.

"Of course I'm mad," Lily blurted. "You killed my flower. Fine. So it was an accident. Okay. I'm over it." Her voice softened considerably when she said this, convincing me that she probably really was over it. "But Parker," she leaned forward into the table with her palms turned up in dismay, "how could you let me blame V?"

I was trying hard to stay easy, so I had to fight the chin muscles that wanted to push themselves forward.

Lily slumped back in her seat and said, "I'm sorry, V."

"It's okay," I said. "You didn't know. And I'm sorry I've been mean sometimes."

I hadn't known I was going to say that until it popped out. But I'd spent a lot of time lately wondering why everybody found it so easy to believe I was a liar and a creep. And I remembered some nasty stuff I might have said.

"Thank you both," said Mary Beth, nodding approvingly at Lily and me. "But, Parker, it's not okay. We'll deal with this later."

Talk about a bummer. We went from major soccer-ball celebration to Parker's no-way-out-of-it prison sentence.

Poor guy. School was going to be out next week and he would be so grounded.

Parker

"You'll live through this," said Lily, reaching over to turn off the bedside light.

"No, I won't," said Parker from the darkness of his bed. He was going to be grounded from now until the middle of June, and he would miss out on everything.

"Are you still mad?" he asked.

"No. I'm not. Honest. Now go to sleep."

"Do V and Eric hate me?"

"Of course not. Go to sleep."

"Lily?"

"What?"

"Will you help me think of one?"

"One what?"

"You know—one of those amazing facts that nobody else knows?"

"Sure," said Lily.

"Promise?"

"Parker, I said I would. So I will. Now, go to sleep."

"Lily?"

"What!?"

"Will you call me Mud Boy?"

There was a long silence. Lily's covers rustled as she turned over. Parker flipped his pillow over nearer to the edge of the bed and waited.

More silence.

"Lily?"

"What?"

"Are you asleep?"

"Yes."

"No, you're not," said Parker.

"Go to sleep, Mud Boy," said Lily.

Lily

I wake up Sunday morning, wishing I had a good science project. Parker is already up, getting dressed for Sunday school.

I pick up the crumpled sheet of newspaper on the floor by my bed and read the "Hands Down Shakedown" article. Now that I know V isn't necessarily a liar, I also know that the reporter probably did mess up his facts.

I flip the page over and read "Birth Order Affects Personality." I keep reading.

It's interesting. Firstborns tend to be perfectionists and leaders. Middle kids are peacemakers, comedians. The babies are free spirits. Sometimes they're spoiled.

Then it goes into a lot of detail about how those descriptions can be stereotypes—meaning, not necessarily true. Or they can have variations, like some second children are quiet, or innovative. I make a mental note to look up "innovative" in the dictionary.

Bigger words start popping up, like "propensity," "manipulative," and "nuanced." And I can't totally follow it anymore, but it makes me think about who I am.

Firstborn. Leader. Idea person. I'm nodding my head as I read, thinking yep, that's me. Then it hits me like a train wreck. No metaphor intended.

I'm *not* the firstborn! Am I?

I mean, I was born first. But now I'm the third oldest. Or second youngest. And then my brain starts to spin.

I think about Eric—comedian turned into leader-guy. Or V. She got older when Frank married Mom because she had me to boss around. But she thinks Mom treats her like a little kid. So, did she get older *and* younger? Which way did she go when Ben died? And what happened to the personality stamped on the first V when she turned into V3?

For a minute, my brain aches like I'm doing word problems in math. I've always known that we got shuffled, but who knew that our personalities got jumbled up, too?

I decide to make a chart to help me track who we were, and who we are now, and who we might be before this whole rearranging thing is finally over. I do me in green ink, V in red, Parker in blue, and Eric, of course, is in black. Right away the poster looks like a road map, with lines going from leader, to shy, to baby brat, to peacemaker, and back again.

I look at it and laugh out loud. The chart is a joke. No help at all. I'm three people now. Maybe four.

"What's funny?" asks Mom, sticking her head in the door.

"Nothing," I say, and wonder if I'm turning into older-Eric-kid, who doesn't talk to parents.

"Hurry up and get dressed," says Mom.

"I can't go to Sunday school today," I say, hoping I can use a last-born trick I just read about—the one called manipulation, which, I think, means, *fooling your parents without telling a flat-out lie.*

"Are you sick?" she asks.

"No. I've got to rework my science project. It's due tomorrow."

I start to add that the reason it had gotten wrecked in the first place was because she wouldn't let anyone eat cicadas. But I'm afraid she'll just remind me that another reason we lost soccer-ball profits is that I forgot to allow for sales tax.

"Well," she says. "Okay."

Okay? Just like that? I don't have to go to Sunday school? Wow.

"You're old enough to decide some things like that for yourself," she adds.

I sit on my bed in total disbelief for a whole five minutes after she's gone. That major surprise calls for one more line on my chart. One green ink pen tracking helpless baby all the way to responsible grown-up.

I decide the chart needs a name, so I pick out a purple marker and write "Who Am I Now?" at the top of the poster.

And then it hits me.

Right in front of me sits the beginning of one killer, A+ science project.

Parker

Everybody started cramming themselves into Eric's hearse—Eric, V, Parker, and Lily. They all had on their RPS T-shirts that Mom and Frank had secretly ordered for them weeks ago. There probably would've been enough room for all of them and the soccer balls, but Frank shouted, "No way!" and made everyone get out because there were only two sets of seat belts.

Eric had his learner's permit, not his license, so Frank had to ride with him to pick up the balls. Everyone else stayed home, spreading the shipping materials out on the new kitchen table.

Parker had been alone and grounded for two weeks, bored out of his head. He'd spent a lot of time trying to think up something awesome that no one else knew. Lily had tried to help him, just like she'd promised, but they were all Lily-sounding facts. Things like, did you know that nothing rhymes with the word "month"?

He was tired of thinking, and sick of being grounded. But now, having everybody at home and working on the same project felt almost like Christmas.

Lily's "Who Am I Now?" science poster covered the refrigerator door where everyone could see it. She'd gotten a B+.

Mrs. Finley said the idea was an A+, but it looked like it had been done in a hurry. Lily didn't mind—it was still the best science grade she'd ever gotten.

Parker couldn't get over the fact that, according to that chart, he was two or three different people now. Like magic. Or triplets.

"Pass the tape," said Lily.

"Okay," said V. "Do you want to hear my new CD later?"

"Sure," said Lily.

Frank and Eric banged into the room carrying twenty soccer balls. One box crunched into the door and tore the screen.

"Oops. Sorry. Eric made me do it," Frank kidded.

"Did not."

"Did, too."

"Boys," Mom scolded, but she looked happy.

"Thanks for all the help—Dad, Mary Beth. And for the T-shirts," said Eric. "We can finish the mailing part."

"It's all yours," said Frank, dismissing everybody with a friendly wave. He and Mom wandered into the den to read boring stuff.

"Can you reach the mailing labels?" Eric asked.

Lily slid them across the table.

Parker thought about the letters he used to get from his dad. "Do you ever hear from your mom?" he asked V and Eric.

"Not much," said Eric.

"She's moved on," said V. "How about *your* dad?"

"Hardly ever."

Quietly and carefully, Lily lowered four soccer balls into a bigger box. Parker wiggled them around to make them fit better. Eric and V filled out labels.

"Frank's cool," said Parker.

"So's Mary Beth," said V.

"Our family's a mess," said Lily.

"Duh," said V, pointing to the chart.

Everyone looked at the tangle of squiggly lines that Lily had drawn on her science project—the one that showed the new and not necessarily improved everybody.

"You know," said Parker, gazing up at the jumbled snarl of colors, "I don't feel *that* messy."

Lily and Eric and V exchanged weird looks, like maybe they *did* feel that messy.

"Well," said Eric, staring at the crisscrossing lines and rubbing his chin like a fake genius. "I definitely don't feel as messy as I used to."

V thought a minute, looked surprised, then nodded.

"Yeah. I guess," said Lily. "Me, either."

Parker glanced triumphantly around the table.

"I did it!" he yelled, thumping his chest.

"Did what?" asked Eric, bending over to wind packing tape around a finished box.

"Told all of you something you didn't know!"

"You're crazy," said Lily. "What didn't we know?"

"That you're not that messy anymore," said Parker, pointing to the poster. "And you didn't even know it until right this exact second. Until I told you. Did you? Huh? Did you? No, you totally did not. Yes!"

ERIC

Journal Entry #184

Parker is one smart little kid.

I'm not that messy anymore. Who knew?

Even V might be right—about Dad and me.

Maybe.

I *am* easy.

I can feel it.

Lily

V is easy.

Well . . . easier.

And I'm younger. *And* older.

Eric smiles more.

And Parker is smarter than any of us knew.

Furthermore, I, Lily, have a killer idea. "Let's raise more money," I say to everybody.

They all stare at me.

Eric, V, and Parker are sprawled across our back steps, acting happy that it's summer. A yellow sprinkler throws long, lazy arcs of water across our garden. Parker is picking at a fresh scab on his knee. The soccer balls are on their way to Iraq.

"We can buy soccer uniforms for the same kids we sent the balls to," I explain.

"Yeah?" says Eric, shifting from his right elbow to his left. "How?"

"RPS?" asks V.

"I don't know. Maybe." I plop down on the bottom step. "Or something new."

Parker picks up an ant that's crawling past his foot. "Are ants non-allergic?" he asks.

"Sure," says Eric. "People eat chocolate-covered ones."

"Cool!" exclaims Parker. "I'll make Insect-insides Two—the sequel!"

"I know!" I say, jumping up. "Let's call them Bug Bites!"

"An ant is not a bug," says V.

"Yes, it is," I answer.

"No, it's not."

"Then what is it?"

"An insect."

"Same thing," I say.

"Hmm," says V.

"Who cares?" I say. "This'll be fun."

Three voices overlap.

"Yeah."

"Awesome."

"Yes!"